A Wedding to Murder For

A Charlie Kingsley Novella

Other books by Michele Pariza Wacek
MPWNovels.com/books

More *Charlie Kingsley Mysteries:* (cozy mysteries)
A Grave Error (a free prequel novel)
The Murder Before Christmas (Book 1)
Ice Cold Murder (Book 2)
Murder Next Door (Book 3)
The Murder of Sleepy Hollow (Book 5)
Red Hot Murder (Book 6)
A Cornucopia of Murder (Book 7)
Arson, Old Lace and Murder (Book 8)
Masquerading as Murder (Book 9)
A Wedding to Murder For (novella)
Loch Ness Murder (novella)
Three French Hens and a Murder (novella)
A Room for Murder (novella)

The Redemption Detective Agency: (cozy mysteries)
The Mysterious Case of the Missing Motive

Riverview Mysteries: (psychological thrillers)
The Stolen Twin
The Taking
Mirror Image
The Thirs Nanny
Today I'll See Her (short story)

Secrets of Redemption series: (psychological thrillers)
It Began With a Lie (Book 1)
This Happened to Jessica (Book 2)
The Evil That Was Done (Book 3)
The Summoning (Book 4)
The Reckoning (Book 5)
The Girl Who Wasn't There (Book 6)
The Room at the Top of the Stairs (Book 7)
The Search (Book 8)
What Wasn't Forgotten (Book 9)
The Secret Diary of Helen Blackstone (novella)

A Wedding to Murder For

A Charley Kingsley Novella

by Michele Pariza Wacek

ISBN 978-1-945363-80-1

For my family, for always believing in me.

Chapter 1

"Charlie!" I immediately recognized the voice. It was my client, Dana. "Thank goodness you're home," she continued, her words careening through the phone in a rush. "I have an emergency, and I need your help."

"An emergency?" I asked, tucking the receiver between my ear and neck, trying not to sound as skeptical as I felt. The last "emergency" Dana had was when she'd insisted her daughter, Cyndi, had been attacked by gargoyles. Of course, there had been no such incident, but that middle-of-the-night call was alarming, not to mention how it interrupted a good night's sleep.

At least this time, it was the middle of the afternoon.

"Yes! You need to come right away. And bring your bag."

"My bag?" I tried not to sigh. "Dana, remember, we talked about this. I'm not a doctor. I sell teas and tinctures."

"Oh, you know what I mean," she said, her words tumbling over one another. "Just come quickly."

"If there's a real emergency, maybe you need to call a real doctor," I said.

"We don't have time for a doctor," Dana said, her voice impatient. "Just get here quickly. And don't forget your bag." The line went dead.

I looked at the phone and then over at Midnight, my black cat, who was watching me from his perch in the warm sun. We were in the kitchen, Midnight curled up in a chair in the sun and me at the counter, which was covered with a variety of dried herbs and flowers I used to create my teas. I grew most of my ingredients myself in my very large backyard. After I created my custom blends, I then delivered them to my clients, as I ran my business out of my house. "If it's a true emergency, she needs a doctor," I said to Midnight.

He looked at me and yawned.

"Yes, I agree. It's probably not," I said. "And I definitely have things I need to be doing. She isn't my only client, you know."

Midnight stared at me.

I sighed. "Fine. I'll go. Only because I want to know what Dana thinks a cup of tea will cure this time."

* * *

"Oh, Charlie. There you are. What took you so long?" Dana asked with a frown. She took a step back and gestured for me to come inside.

"It's only been fifteen minutes," I started to say, but immediately left it there. Dana was clearly not paying any attention to me, as she was examining her nails, instead, which had been professionally polished a delicate pale pink. "Is that a chip?" she muttered. "Well, never mind, no time for it now. Did you bring your bag?"

"If you mean my bag with tea and tincture samples in it, then yes, I brought it," I said.

Dana rolled her eyes dramatically. "Charlie, sometimes you can be so difficult." As usual, Dana was dressed to perfection in a simple-but-elegant red dress accentuated by a single strand of pearls. She bore a passing resemblance to Princess Di and did everything she could to play it up, including the way she styled her hair. I had forgotten how frumpy I sometimes felt next to her, with my worn, mud-stained jeans and oversized green shirt. I reached up to try and tame my wild, brownish-blonde hair and discovered a few remnants of dried flowers and herbs in it.

"Come, she's waiting for you in the living room," Dana said.

"Cyndi?" Cyndi was her teenage daughter, whose fashion sense was the polar opposite of her mom's—Cyndi Lauper, all the way.

"Heavens, no," Dana said, as she started walking through the house. "It's my niece, Anastasia."

"I didn't realize you had a niece," I started to say, but my words were drowned out by loud, petulant voices emerging from the living room.

"No, that's not going to work. Don't you see? It's all ruined. How can we possibly go on?"

Dana's face paled. "Oh, dear. Now what?" she muttered before rushing forward, her heels clacking on the smooth tile. "Anastasia? Dear, what's going on?"

I quickly followed, turning the corner that led to the living room, which revealed quite a scene. A tear-stained young woman sat on the couch, her mascara streaked down her face and her white-blonde curls falling out of a messy ponytail. I suspected she would have been quite attractive in normal situations, but her skin was so red and blotchy and her makeup so smeared, it was hard to see in the moment. On one side of her was a much older, less made-up, more exhausted version of Dana, trying in vain to comfort her. On her other was a third woman, who looked about my age—early thirties, or maybe a little older. She seemed almost as stressed and overwhelmed as the older woman. "Anastasia, I really don't think anyone will be able to tell the difference," she started to say, but Anastasia began shaking her head violently, which dislodged even more long curls.

"Jane, are you kidding me?" she screeched. "*Everyone* will know. The Duckworths are coming! Do you understand what that means? Of course they will know, and they'll probably be laughing at me the entire time." She burst into another round of tears as Jane looked helplessly on. She had mousy brown hair pinned back in a smooth, neat ponytail and wore a no-nonsense beige pantsuit that wasn't particularly flattering.

"Anastasia, honey, what happened?" Dana asked, rushing in to hug the sobbing girl.

"Oh, Aunt Dana, it's ... it's dreadful," Anastasia said between hiccups.

"What? What is?"

Anastasia was too distraught to talk. She flapped her hand toward the coffee table, which was loaded with piles of thick, engraved paper. Dana craned her head back. "Oh, the invitations arrived. Is there a problem with them? Oh ..." she wrinkled her brow. "I thought you had decided on ivory invitations. Those look like ecru."

"See!" Anastasia burst out. Jane's face shifted, as if she wished the floor would open up then and there to swallow her. "I told you everyone would know the difference between ecru and ivory! How could you make such a stupid mistake?"

The other woman—the older Dana—had picked up one of the invitations and was turning it over in her hand. "Dana, how can you tell the difference between ecru and ivory? They're both basically white."

"Oh for heaven's sake, Mary Rose, it's obvious. Just look at it," Dana said as she patted Anastasia's shoulder. "There, there. I'm sure we'll work something out. Is it too late to order new ones?"

Anastasia hiccupped. "If we want them to go out in time, yes."

Dana frowned slightly. "Oh, well. I'm sure we can work it out."

"No, we won't. It's all ruined," Anastasia wailed.

"Well, first, why don't we take a moment to just breathe," Dana suggested. "That's the idea. Take a nice deep breath." Anastasia inhaled deeply, her breath hitching. "Much better. I want to introduce you to Charlie. She's going to fix you right up."

Anastasia raised her watery eyes to me and jerkily nodded her head.

"Oh, are you a doctor?" Jane asked, her voice hopeful. I sensed she might even be crossing her fingers, in the hopes that I brought some good drugs for the miserable bride.

"No, I make custom teas and tinctures," I said.

Jane's face fell.

"They're wonderful," Dana added, extracting herself from Anastasia. "I couldn't sleep without them. Here, let me show you where the kitchen is."

"I know where ..." I started to say, but Dana grabbed me by the arm, quite painfully, I might add, and yanked me into the hallway. "We'll be right back," she sang out as she hauled me toward the kitchen.

"Do you see the problem?" she hissed in my ear. "Anastasia has been beside herself with all the wedding planning, and the closer we come to the wedding, the worse she gets. She's going to be catatonic on her wedding day, at this rate. Can you give her something to calm her down?"

"I have just the thing," I said, thinking of my lavender and chamomile blend. Normally, I would recommend that tea for right before bed, but based on what I saw, I had a feeling I needed my most potent blend. In fact, I decided to amp up the relaxation qualities with one of my tinctures.

Dana shot me a relieved smile and loosened her grip on my arm. "I knew I could count on you. She's a good girl, but …" Dana shook her head. "This is all very stressful on her, marrying into the Duckworth family. And my sister is no help. She never did understand how to move in those circles." Her voice, the one she used when she was in British Royalty mode, was haughty. I didn't have the heart to tell her that dressing as Princess Di and faithfully following the Royal Family in celebrity gossip magazines did not make one an expert.

"Well, it's a good thing Anastasia has you," I said solemnly. "In fact, if you want to go back to the living room, I'll take care of the tea and bring it in as soon as it's ready."

Dana pressed a hand against her chest. "Oh, I feel like you've lifted a huge weight off my shoulders. Thank you." She turned, and I continued my way into the kitchen, listening to the heels of her pumps clicking away on the tile floor.

I expected the kitchen to be empty, but instead, I discovered Cyndi, Dana's daughter, there. She was eating a peach as she leaned against the counter, dressed in ripped jean shorts and a hot-pink top.

"Ah, she sucked you into the madness, too," she said in greeting as peach juice dripped down her arm. She lapped it up with a tiny tongue, reminding me of a cat. Like her mother, she had a full face of makeup on, and her hair was done, but that was where the similarities ended.

"I'm surprised you're not in the living room helping with the wedding planning," I said, putting my bag on the counter and rifling through it to find the tea I wanted. "Isn't that the dream of every teenage girl? To get married?"

Cyndi rolled her eyes, as only a teenager could. "I have no intention of getting married," she said archly. "And if I do, I'll probably elope and do it on a beach somewhere. Or maybe Vegas."

"You don't want to get married here, and have your mom plan a nice, big wedding?" I asked as I filled the modern-shaped black tea kettle with water. Like the rest of the house, Dana had designed it with an ultra-modern, ultra-sleek look.

"Very funny," Cyndi said. "If I wanted that, I'd be in the living room right now."

I got the water boiling and went hunting for mugs. "I'm curious," I said, switching subjects. "Is your cousin always so … high-strung?"

Cyndi took another bite of her peach, her brow furrowed as she thought. "I don't know if that's the word I would use to describe her. She's always been interested in clothes and hair … that sort of stuff. She and my mom used to spend hours together." She rolled her eyes again. "My mom loved styling her hair and putting on her makeup. But I never saw Anastasia as the Bridezilla type. My bad." She took another bite of her peach. "Although," she continued with her mouth full, "it's possible she's acting like she has the worst case of PMS because she's psyched herself out over who she's marrying."

"A Duckworth, I'm gathering?" The Duckworths were the wealthiest and most influential family in Riverview, Wisconsin, which was about forty-five minutes away from Redemption. While they had their hand in nearly every type of business, they were most known for medical and pharmaceuticals. Even though the majority of people in Redemption didn't concern themselves much with the day-to-day happenings of the Duckworths, everyone knew who they were.

Cyndi shot me a look. "Barely. And I do mean barely. I think James's mother is some sort of cousin once removed or something. But, yeah, there will likely be Duckworths at the wedding, which is probably part of why she's so nuts now. That, and her fiancé is going to be a surgeon."

"Oh?" The water was boiling, so I started pouring it into a mug. "You think she's trying to impress her fiancé?"

Cyndi shrugged. "All I know is if you really want to see high-strung, take a look at that whole family. They're all wound way too tightly." She tossed her peach pit into the garbage and wiped her fingers on her jean shorts. "I wouldn't want to marry into it, that's for sure. Way too much pressure. Definitely a heart attack waiting to happen. Mark my words—one of them is going to die an early death," she said, her voice ominous as she sauntered out the door.

Even though I wanted to dismiss what Cyndi said as the words of an overly dramatic teenager, something unpleasant twinged in my gut.

No, I'm not going there, I told myself firmly. *I'm here to make a cup of tea for Anastasia, and that's it.*

Chapter 2

"I can't believe you're now part of the Hartmann wedding party," Pat said, her voice envious. We were sitting at my kitchen table, cups of tea and a plate of my famous chocolate chip cookies in front of us. Pat had just deposited Tiki, her toy poodle, on the floor so she could sniff around. Midnight, who was sleeping in his usual spot on the chair next to the window, was keeping a close eye on her. I, in turn, was keeping a close eye on him, as I didn't want him torturing the little dog (Midnight weighed more than she did). Luckily, he seemed content to watch her from his perch.

"I wouldn't exactly say I'm part of the wedding party," I said.

"Didn't you just say you now have an open invitation to all of the wedding events, including the cake tasting tomorrow?" Pat asked.

"Well, yes, but …"

"And didn't the bride tell you she was depending on you, and therefore, that you would have a special reserved spot at all these wedding events?"

"Yes, but …"

"And don't you now have a designated title?"

"It's a made-up title," I said. "There's no such thing as a 'Bride Whisperer.'"

"And that's a travesty," Pat said. "Every bride should have one."

"Besides, that's not what Anastasia called me. Her mother said it," I clarified. When I had returned to the living room, tea in hand, Jane had immediately stood up and gestured for me to sit next to the visibly distraught bride-to-be, although she was at least no longer openly sobbing. I hadn't particularly wanted to sit next to Anastasia, as I could just feel myself getting sucked into her family drama. But I also couldn't help but feel a little sorry for her. So, I handed her the tea and sat down next to her, rubbing her back and giving her pointers on breathing. I wasn't sure what I expected to happen, but to my surprise (and I think everyone else's in the room), Anastasia calmed down considerably and became much more reasonable about the invitation snafu. It wasn't long after that I found myself in my new role as Anastasia's Bride Whisperer.

I still hadn't quite decided how I felt about it.

"If the mother of the bride is giving you a title, trust me, you're an official member of the wedding party," Pat said. "Which should mean you get a plus one for the wedding, right?" She waggled her eyebrows up and down at me.

Pat was a good decade or so older than me, and the best way to describe her was "round." She was plump, with a round face, round, black-rimmed glasses, and short, no-nonsense brown hair that was turning gray. She had been one of my first tea customers, and had since become one of my best friends, as well as my partner in crime-solving—although I had some mixed emotions about being Redemption's resident amateur sleuth.

"I can't ask if I can bring a guest to the wedding," I said, horrified by the idea of such a breach of etiquette.

"Why not?" Pat demanded, reaching for a cookie. "Are they paying you for your whispering services?"

"Well, no," I said.

"Then it sounds like a plus-one situation," Pat said, as if the matter was settled. "Which is a good thing, because there's no way I'm missing this wedding. I'm not completely sure if Dana and I are close enough to make the cut, and I don't know Mary Rose outside of basic encounters, so I have no clue if I'd score an invitation."

"What exactly were you going to do if Dana didn't invite you, and I didn't have a plus one?" I asked.

Pat straightened her back and squared her shoulders. "Whatever it takes."

"What, like crash the wedding?"

"I just said, 'whatever it takes,'" Pat repeated. "Do you know the reception is going to be at the Redemption Supper Club? Apparently, they rented out the entire restaurant. Imagine! The

Redemption Supper Club! I've been there exactly two times in my life, and one of them was when Richard proposed."

The Redemption Supper Club was one of the town's most famous landmarks. Ironically, it wasn't located in Redemption proper, but a few miles outside of it, off of Angel's Lake. The views were gorgeous and the food outstanding, made by a Michelin Star chef, which of course was reflected in the prices. Most of the locals only went there for special occasions. I personally had yet to experience it.

"Pretty swanky," I said.

"Well, when you're marrying into the Duckworth family, swanky comes with the territory," Pat said. "Which is why, if you think I'm giving up this opportunity to have a free meal of that caliber, you are sadly mistaken."

"Duly noted. I'll make sure Dana knows about my plus one," I said drily. "Man, renting out the entire Redemption Supper Club. That can't be cheap."

"I would say not," Pat agreed, taking a bite of cookie.

"I know she's marrying into the Duckworth family, or at least a cousin or something, but doesn't the bride's family typically pay for the wedding?" I asked.

Pat paused mid-chew. "You don't think they can afford it?"

"I have no idea. It's not like I asked how much is in their checking account." I pictured Mary Rose and Anastasia. Neither was dressed expensively, but that didn't mean they didn't have money. Plenty of wealthy people lived in jeans and tee shirts. Still, there was something about the whole situation that made me think Anastasia was marrying into money, rather than having her own. "If they don't have the money for a super-expensive wedding, which this seems to be, that's got to be adding to the stress."

"Maybe they figure it will pay off once Anastasia is part of the Duckworth family," Pat said. "They certainly wouldn't be the first to think it. I also heard that Anastasia is marrying a doctor."

"I think he's still in medical school, but yes, he's studying to be a surgeon."

"Oh, a *surgeon*," Pat said, exaggerating the word. "Makes sense. After all, if you're a Duckworth, you can't just be a run-of-the mill doctor, no siree. Only being a *surgeon* will do."

"A specialist might be acceptable, as well," I said. "But regardless, I suspect there's a lot of pressure on Anastasia. I don't know what she went to school for, but if it's not something like a doctor or lawyer, she might already feel like a second-class citizen."

"Hence why she's going overboard with the wedding planning," Pat said.

"And having meltdowns over the smallest details, like the wrong shade of white for the invitations," I added.

Pat reached for another cookie. "Yeah, when you put it like that, it's almost easy to feel sorry for her."

"Almost," I agreed, thinking of the exhaustion and overwhelm on both Jane, the wedding planner's, and her mother's face. "No question this is hard on everyone."

"Well, not me," Pat said smugly. "I'm going to get to enjoy a delicious meal at the Redemption Supper Club without any of the unpleasantness of being part of the wedding party."

"Careful," I said. "I might decide to bring someone else, instead."

Pat's eyes widened in horror. "You wouldn't dare."

Chapter 3

"Oh, thank goodness," Dana said when she saw me standing on her front porch loaded with tea. She grabbed my arm and yanked me inside. "We have a major breakdown brewing. I'm worried Anastasia is going to cancel the wedding!"

"What happened now?" I didn't think the cake tasting had started yet, nor could I imagine what else could have gotten Anastasia so upset that she would consider canceling. "Was there another problem with the invitations?"

"No, this is worse." There was a strain around Dana's eyes that wasn't there the last time I'd seen her. "Anastasia found James having lunch with his ex-girlfriend."

"What?" That did sound more serious than an invitation mishap. "Is he cheating on her?"

Dana shook her head. "I don't think so. His mother was there, too."

"Wait, his *mother* was having lunch with him and his ex-girlfriend?" This wedding was getting stranger and stranger.

Dana opened her mouth to respond, but loud voices from deeper inside the house interrupted her. She pressed her lips together. "I better go. Just please make the tea. Extra strong."

"Okay," I said, although I wasn't sure if it was possible to make my herbal tea strong enough to combat an ex-girlfriend on the warpath. Maybe I needed to revisit Anastasia seeing a doctor—one who could prescribe Valium.

As I headed to the kitchen, the voices became even louder. "Anastasia, please," a male voice said. "I love YOU. I'm marrying YOU. You know that Bridget is an old family friend. There's nothing between us."

"But why would you even have lunch with her then?" Anastasia demanded. I passed by an open door that led to a good-sized utility room. Anastasia was standing in the middle of it with a man who seemed to be about her age. He wasn't bad-looking, with his wheat-colored hair and gray eyes, but his nose was a little too big in comparison to the rest of his features.

"Charlie," Anastasia said, interrupting whatever answer James was attempting to form. "I'm so glad you're here. Did you bring the tea?"

"I did," I said. "I'm going to go make it right now."

She pressed a hand against her chest. "Oh, good. I really need it. Along with some alcohol!" Anastasia looked a little more put together than the last time. Her makeup wasn't smeared with tears yet, which was a bit of a surprise, considering, and she was dressed in a white silk blouse with pressed black pants. "Oh, and this is James, my fiancé." She spat out the word "fiancé," and James winced.

"Oh, you're the tea lady," James said. "I've heard a lot about you."

"Likewise," I said, although I hadn't really heard much at all, other than he was a Duckworth and studying to be a surgeon. Still, it seemed like the polite thing to say. "Let me go make the tea, and I'll be right out."

"Okay. We'll wait to start the cake tasting until you're done," Anastasia said.

"You don't have to," I said, thinking the sooner the cake tasting started, the sooner I could leave what felt like a very uncomfortable gathering.

Anastasia offered me a brittle smile. "I insist. It's the least I can do for my true friends." She gave James the side-eye, and he winced again.

"Anastasia, please," he started to say as I hurried to the kitchen. I certainly didn't want to be the one holding things up. Stepping into the kitchen, I saw Jane, who was chugging a glass of champagne.

"Oh," she choked, spilling some on her beige pantsuit. It looked like the exact same one she'd had on when I met her. Her cheeks turned bright red. "I'm such a klutz."

"Sorry," I said. "I didn't mean to scare you."

She threw me a faint smile before gathering up two gold buckets filled with ice and champagne bottles. "It's fine. I have to go finish setting up."

"Of course," I said, moving quickly to the stove to get the water boiling. I made the tea in record time and went in search of Anastasia. I found her in the dining room with the rest of the guests.

"Charlie," she called out as she made a beeline toward me. "You are a lifesaver."

I handed her the mug as I quickly scanned the crowd. Dana and Jane were there, along with Cyndi and Mary Rose. An older, balding man with a slight paunch was standing next to Mary Rose, who I assumed was Anastasia's father. I could see the resemblance, especially around the lips and chin.

"Oh, that hit the spot," Anastasia breathed before turning to wave to Jane, who was hovering in the back. "We can get started now," she called out. Jane nodded, a fake smile plastered across her face.

Anastasia tucked a hand in the crook of my arm. "Charlie, you're going to sit next to me," she announced to no one in particular.

"That sounds great," I said, wondering if my smile looked like Jane's.

She led me to the dining room table, which was already laid out with napkins, plates, forks, and tall, thin glasses of champagne. James followed us. "Are we getting started now?"

"Isn't that what I just said?" Anastasia snapped, pushing him aside.

James swallowed hard before heading back toward the crowd, presumably to help them find their spots at the table.

It took a few moments, but eventually, everyone was seated. James was sitting on Anastasia's other side, while Dana and Mary Rose sat across from us, next to a tall, regal-looking woman whose hair was pinned up in a stylish bun. She wore a navy-blue silk sheath with a simple gold necklace and what appeared to be diamond studs in her ears.

"Blanche," she introduced herself. "I'm James's mother. I'm also the one who is apparently to blame for this whole sordid mess."

"Don't be silly," Anastasia said, her voice a little too high and strained. I nudged the mug of tea toward her. She took the hint and gulped down a few more swallows.

Blanche flashed me an apologetic smile. "Bridget is an old family friend," she said. "She and James were practically raised together. It didn't even occur to me how it would look to ask her to join James and me for lunch. But I can see why some might find it inappropriate."

"It is a little ... unusual," I said. "What was the occasion, if you don't mind my asking?"

Blanche looked a little embarrassed. "James was trying to decide where to go for his honeymoon, and last year, Bridget had gone on this incredible cruise in the Greek Isles. I thought that would make for a wonderful honeymoon, so I invited Bridget to lunch so James could pick her brain about the trip."

"Oh, well, that's fortunate," I murmured, while trying to reconcile in my head the groom's mother inviting an ex-girlfriend to lunch to help plan her son's honeymoon. That didn't seem the least bit awkward at all.

Blanche must have seen something in my expression, because she leaned forward slightly. "I know it sounds a little ... unorthodox, but truly, James and Bridget are still very good friends. It was a couple years ago when they were dating, and while I would be lying if I said we—and Bridget's parents—weren't excited at the thought of our families becoming permanently connected, as it turned out, they were both too good of friends to make dating work."

"She's like my sister," James said. "And trust me, you don't want to spend the rest of your life with your sister."

Thinking about my own strained relationship with my two sisters, I had to agree.

Blanche's smile was a little frosty. "Yes, in retrospect, our families might have spent a little too much time together, but we're so glad to welcome Anastasia as our future daughter. Aren't we, James?" She turned to the distinguished man sitting next to her, who looked like the spitting image of James Junior, including the size of his nose. He had already drained half the champagne from his flute and looked a little startled to suddenly be the center of attention.

"Absolutely," he boomed as he gestured to Jane to refill his glass.

Jane brought the champagne over, along with the first of the cakes, which was lemon.

"I can't wait for the chocolate," said a plump girl with freckles and red hair. Her name was Denise, and she was Anastasia's maid of honor.

"I'm not sure chocolate is a good choice for a wedding cake," Blanche advised.

Denise's cheeks turned red. "When I get married, I'm definitely having a chocolate cake," she muttered to the piece of lemon cake on her plate.

There was an awkward moment of silence.

"Oh, I do love a good lemon cake," Mary Rose interjected, trying to relieve the awkwardness.

"Exactly," Dana said. "Who doesn't? It's an excellent choice for a wedding."

"But not this one," Anastasia said in disgust, dropping her fork on the plate so it landed with a clatter. "This one is way too lemony. We need something more subtle."

I took a bite, and while lemon cake wasn't my favorite, I thought it tasted fine.

Needless to say, none of the cakes were up to satisfaction. The vanilla was too dry, the chocolate too chocolaty, and the carrot just too "healthy." "Who on Earth wants to eat carrots on their wedding day?" Anastasia asked incredulously.

"The cream cheese frosting is pretty good, though," Denise said, licking her fork.

"We can't have cream cheese frosting on a wedding cake," Anastasia said, aghast.

Denise reached for her champagne flute.

There would be no winner, at this tasting. "None of these are acceptable," Anastasia said flatly. "Truly, Jane, I'm a little disappointed. I thought you had a personal relationship with the baker."

"Sometimes, it takes a few attempts to nail down the right flavor for the bride," Jane said. "Everyone is different."

Anastasia frowned. "I guess. We're going to need another set of cakes to taste. Do you think you can handle that?"

"Of course," Jane said, her smile brittle. "I just need a moment." As she strode out of the room, I saw her grab a half-filled bottle of champagne and take it with her.

Chapter 4

"I'm still having trouble wrapping my head around the groom getting honeymoon pointers from his ex," Pat said as I hunted for a parking spot on Dana's street. We were headed to Anastasia's bridal shower. After hearing my stories, Pat insisted on seeing the bridal party in action. Luckily, Dana was more than open to having Pat attend as a guest. Although I was less sure that the invitation had been extended to Tiki, who sat happily on Pat's lap, neatly groomed and dressed in a sparkling pink shirt with matching pink ribbons. Pat didn't dress her up often, but she said this was a special occasion.

"The whole thing was weird," I said, quickly navigating to the side of the road and parking the car. We were about half a block from Dana's house, but the weather was perfect—mid-seventies, with a light breeze and low humidity—so a short stroll wouldn't be an issue. "Personally, I think the future mother-in-law is behind it. She seemed pretty disappointed that James was no longer dating this Bridget person, so I'm wondering if she was trying to show James that there is still time to leave Anastasia and go back to Bridget."

"Well, with the way Anastasia is acting, I can hardly blame her," Pat said, getting out of the car and fumbling around to organize her purse, Tiki, and the present. "She sounds like she's lost her mind."

"She does seem like she's on the edge of a nervous breakdown," I agreed. "Although I do wonder how much is her versus everyone else. It's got to be stressful, knowing your future mother-in-law would so much rather her son marry someone else that she's inviting past girlfriends to have lunch with them."

"Yeah, that's tough," Pat said, finally straightening up and eyeing me. "It wouldn't kill you to help, you know."

"I have to take care of myself," I said. "Being a Bride Whisperer is a tough job. I can't be distracted by all these other details."

Pat gave me look. "Is that why we had to park a half-mile away?"

"A half-block away," I corrected. "And look at the cars. Do you see any spots?"

Pat glanced around, as if suddenly noticing all the cars lining both sides of the quiet neighborhood street. "Goodness," she said. "I know Dana has a big house, but this seems excessive even for her."

"That's why she's holding it in the backyard."

"Good thing it's such a beautiful day," Pat said.

We made our way up to the porch and rang the bell. Mary Rose opened the door, her expression turning to relief when she saw me. "Oh, thank heavens," she said. "Everything is falling apart."

"Already?" I asked, stepping inside. Pat and Tiki, who was happily sniffing around, followed. I didn't think Mary Rose even noticed the dog.

Mary Rose shook her head. "It's Bridget," she said in a loud whisper. "She's here."

I blinked at her. "Bridget? Ex-girlfriend, Bridget?"

"Yes, that's the one."

I glanced at Pat, who had the same question mirrored in her eyes. "But I don't understand. How did she get invited? Who invites the groom's ex-girlfriend to a bridal shower?"

"I have no idea," Mary Rose said, although her pursed lips and sharp expression said otherwise. It appeared she had allowed her younger sister to do her makeup and hair for the occasion, as she now also bore a passing resemblance to a much older Princess Di.

"I guess I better go make the tea," I said.

Mary Rose waved vaguely toward the back of the house. "You'll find Anastasia back there. Everyone else should already be out in the yard."

"I'll head out there," Pat said as I started making my way to the kitchen.

As I neared the utility room, I could hear what sounded like Anastasia's voice. "How could you let this happen? Are you trying to sabotage my wedding? Or are you just that incompetent?"

My heart sank. I had a bad feeling who was stuck enduring the brunt of Anastasia's displeasure. Sure enough, Anastasia and Jane were huddled in the utility room, Anastasia looking furious and Jane appearing more than a little beaten down.

Anastasia's face cleared when she saw me. "Oh, thank goodness, Charlie. You're finally here. I'm SO glad to see you. I've had a such an awful day."

"Let me go get the tea started, and you can tell me all about it," I said. "Why don't you go freshen up while I do that?"

She nodded, the red splotches slowly leaving her cheeks. It didn't appear like she had been crying, which was good, but at some point during her tirade, her lipstick had smeared, and her mascara had flecked off. "That's a good idea. Give me a moment to catch my breath."

"I'll just ... go see about the guests," Jane said, edging away from Anastasia. She shot me a grateful look before disappearing down the hall, moving as fast as she could without it looking too obvious.

Anastasia's lips thinned as she watched her go. "She's terrible," she said to me in a low voice. "I have no idea how she's managed to keep any clients, let alone stay in business."

"It's not easy being a wedding planner," I offered, keeping my voice neutral. "How did you hear about her?"

"Blanche recommended her," Anastasia said, a tinge of disgust in her voice. "So I, of course, immediately hired her. I didn't even look for anyone else." She shook her head, her carefully styled blonde curls spilling across her face. "That was a mistake."

Somehow, I wasn't surprised to find out Blanche was behind Jane's hiring, although what I still wasn't sure about was how much of Jane's "screwups" were actually mistakes. Anastasia seemed fairly prone to having panic attacks. But even if Jane was a perfectly fine wedding planner, she clearly wasn't a good fit for Anastasia, which made me wonder if that was the reason why Blanche recommended her in the first place. Still, it could have just been a coincidence. "How does Blanche know about her? Has she worked with her on another project?"

"I think she was the wedding planner for one of her friend's weddings," Anastasia said. "She said she was highly recommended and in great demand, and if I could get her, I should snatch her up. So that's what I did. And you see the results." She waved her arms in a large, encompassing gesture.

"Hmm," I murmured noncommittally. "I'll get the tea taken care of while you take a moment for yourself, okay? I'll be right back."

She nodded, and I hurried to the kitchen. This time, it was empty, although it was already full of dirty dishes and large platters of appetizers—miniature quiches and stuffed mushrooms—along with champagne bottles just waiting to be put out. I was able to locate a large clean mug in the back of the cupboard, and once the tea was prepared, I went looking for Anastasia.

I found her in the backyard, makeup immaculate, having taken my "quick bathroom break" suggestion to heart. She was holding an untouched flute of champagne and talking to a truly stunning girl. She had long, thick, strawberry-blonde curls that hung to the middle of her back and large, startling green eyes. "Oh, Charlie," Anastasia called out, waving a manicured hand. "Let me introduce you to Bridget."

"I've heard so much about you," Bridget said with a wide smile. "It's so great to meet a real-life Bride Whisperer."

"I was surprised as anyone to discover I had that talent," I replied. While there was no question that Anastasia was very pretty, in contrast with Bridget, she looked positively plain. I could see why she would have some concern around James spending a lot of time with his drop-dead gorgeous ex.

I handed Anastasia the tea, who took the mug from me eagerly with one hand, the other still holding the champagne. She immediately took a sip as Bridget watched her, her face curious.

"That must be some tea," Bridget said.

"Trust me, it's so much better at relaxing me than this," Anastasia said, lifting her champagne flute. "It gives me a similar buzzy feeling without the downside of alcohol."

Bridget lifted a perfectly manicured eyebrow. "Really? That's hard to believe. I may have to give it a try someday."

"The secret is valerian, along with a few other ingredients," I said. "But if you'd like some tea of your own, just give me a call. I make and sell custom blends."

"And they're wonderful," Anastasia said, craning her neck around. "Give me a second … I'm going to put this down." She gestured with the champagne glass as she moved toward a large table covered with a white tablecloth and fine china place settings, leaving me alone with Bridget.

"Beautiful day for a bridal shower," I said, feeling a little inane. I was trying to figure out how I could ask her how she ended up with an invitation, and why she would possibly come, without sounding terribly rude.

Bridget took a sip of champagne and looked around. "Yes. Dana did a fabulous job."

I agreed. Along with the immaculately groomed rose bushes and flower beds, she had erected a huge white tent in the center of the yard and added carefully arranged food and alcohol stations throughout. All the gifts were heaped on a table under the tent, which was surrounded by an army of chairs. At the far end of the yard, I spotted Pat talking to Blanche. Blanche appeared to be admiring Tiki, although it also could have been simple amazement around someone having the audacity to bring a dog to a bridal shower. Seeing as she was likely the one who brought Bridget, she probably shouldn't be judging, though. Anastasia had started up a conversation with Denise and another girl, so it appeared, at least for the moment, that it was just me and Bridget.

"So, how do you know Anastasia?" I asked.

Bridget's green eyes carefully studied me over the rim of her champagne flute. "Actually, I'm a friend of James's. We used to date. But, as Anastasia's Bride Whisperer, I suspect you know that already."

I couldn't help but smile. "You got me," I said.

She smiled brightly in return. "So, what you're really probably wondering is why, as the ex-girlfriend, I would be here."

"That question did cross my mind."

She flashed her dazzling smile again. "The truth is not that mysterious. My family and Blanche's family go way back. As toddlers, James and I used to play together. We're still close. And, yes, we dated for about six months or so, but it didn't work out, and we parted as friends. As for why I'm here, Blanche invited me as her guest."

I stared at her in surprise. "She did?"

Bridget nodded and sipped more champagne. "It's no big deal. She told me she cleared it with Anastasia first, and she was fine with it."

That was news to me, and probably Mary Rose, Dana, and maybe even Anastasia, herself. "That was thoughtful of Blanche to do that," I said. "But it still doesn't explain why she invited you in the first place, even with Anastasia's blessing. It just seems a little … odd, to have you here. No offense, of course."

"It probably does look that way from your standpoint," Bridget agreed, her voice charming on the surface, but underneath, I detected a condescending bite. "But Blanche isn't just a friend. She's also a client."

"A client?" I couldn't possibly imagine what sort of client Blanche would be.

"Yes, I'm going into fashion, and I've been helping Blanche with her wardrobe. She especially wanted me to design an ensemble for both her and James Senior for the wedding. Part of my job is to not only design outfits that suit them personally, but that also fit the overall brand of the wedding. Hence, why Blanche thought it would be a good idea for me to come with her today … so I could start getting a feel for the style of the wedding."

"Oh, that makes sense," I said, and in a way, it did. My own family was quite wealthy; I even had a trust fund that had been set up from my grandparents, so I well understood how wealthy people often did things that seemed peculiar to "normal" people.

But there still seemed something off about it. Whether it was her manner or her tone, something about what she was telling me didn't completely jive with her words.

I wondered what she was hiding.

"Excuse me. Everyone. Excuse me. Could I have your attention?" Dana was standing under the tent, tapping her champagne flute with a spoon. "Great. Thank you all for coming today. We've got an exciting day planned with some fun games and a truly to-die-for cake, but first, I wanted to make a toast. So, please, if you can find a glass or get a refill ..." She held up her champagne flute.

Bridget eyed me. "Oh no, you didn't get any champagne. Here, I'll fetch one for you. I need a refill, anyway."

"That's okay. I don't drink much," I started to say, but Bridget was already weaving through the crowd toward one of the waitstaff. Anastasia was standing nearby, and as I watched, I saw Bridget crash into her, sloshing the tea in her hand.

"Oh, I'm such a klutz." I could hear her say over the crowd. "I'm so sorry, Anastasia."

"That's okay," Anastasia said through gritted teeth.

"Did I make you spill on your pretty dress? Let me look." Bridget stepped toward her, but Anastasia backed away.

"No, it's fine. I didn't spill. Don't worry about it," Anastasia insisted, using one hand to brush her dress. It was pale blue with white flowers, so luckily, even if she had gotten any tea on it, it wouldn't have shown on the pattern.

"Where's your champagne?" Bridget asked Anastasia. "Do you need me to get you a glass? You can't toast with tea, for heaven's sake."

"I'm fine," Anastasia started to say, but a commotion on the other side of the yard interrupted her.

A crowd of women, including Pat, were all focused on something I couldn't see. "Is she okay?" I heard one of them ask.

"I don't know ... she doesn't look right," another said.

"Call an ambulance." That voice was Pat, and I saw her muscle her way through the crowd as Tiki began to bark. "Hurry. I don't think she's breathing."

"What's going on?" Dana was asking.

I ran over and pushed my way through the women. Pat was kneeling on the ground, her back to me, blocking whoever was lying there. Tiki was running around in circles, barking her little head off. "Pat? What's going on?" I yelled between the barks.

Pat turned her head, and I could see the anguish in her eyes. "Call an ambulance. Hurry!" Her eyes focused on me. "It's that wedding planner. I think she's dead!"

Chapter 5

"I'm afraid to even ask why you're here," Officer Brandon Wyle said to me. We were in the kitchen, while the rest of the guests huddled in the living room and dining room under the watchful eyes of other officers. The crime scene investigators were securing the scene.

Wyle and I had often sparred about my sleuthing. He preferred me to leave the investigating to the professionals, rather than doing it myself on the side as a hobby. I actually preferred that, as well. Focusing solely on my garden and creating teas and tinctures for my clients while keeping as low a profile as possible was all I really wanted. I honestly didn't want to be in the spotlight any more than I had to be.

Much to my surprise, though, I'd inadvertently discovered my knack for solving crime. And since my clients also seemed to have a knack for getting themselves into trouble on that front, it appeared to be a match made in heaven. At least for my clients. Wyle would vehemently disagree.

Wyle was a good-looking guy with a thick head of dark hair that perpetually looked in need of a cut, dark eyes, high cheekbones, a square-cut jawline, and a lean build—although his good looks were currently marred by his incredibly obvious frown.

"I'm Anastasia's Bride Whisperer," I informed him archly.

He raised an eyebrow. "A 'Bride Whisperer'? Is that even a thing?"

"Apparently, it is now," I said.

He closed his eyes briefly, as if this brand-new case was already giving him a headache. "I know I'm going to regret asking this, but what does a Bride Whisperer do?"

"Well, in this particular case, keep the bride from having a nervous breakdown," I said.

"Is it working?"

"She hasn't had one yet," I said. "At least, nothing serious, although I haven't been able to do much with the anxiety attacks and occasional outbursts. I'm working on it, though."

His lips quirked up. "Has Anastasia had any anxiety attacks or outbursts today?"

This was the question I was dreading. I was still hoping that whatever caused Jane to collapse was something completely out of everyone's control. "How is Jane?" The EMT had taken her away in an ambulance with lights and sirens blaring, so despite Pat's pronouncement at the scene, I had hope she might still pull through.

His eyes narrowed. "You're avoiding the question."

"Yes, because I'm concerned about Jane. I'm hoping she recovers."

He tapped his pen against his notebook. "Not good. The last I heard from the hospital, they don't think she's going to make it."

"Oh no." I had been a little afraid that might be the answer, after seeing Jane on the ground. But I had also been hoping the doctors would find some way to save her. "Do they know what's wrong with her? Does she have a medical condition, or anything like that?"

He gave me a hard look. "We won't know for sure until after they've run some tests, but right now, it appears she was poisoned."

My eyes went wide. "Poisoned? Someone tried to kill the wedding planner?"

"That's exactly what it looks like, which is why we're taking this time to interview everyone and examine the scene while it's fresh."

My head spun. Anastasia yelling at Jane suddenly took on even graver importance, and while it was true Anastasia wasn't happy with Jane's wedding-planning abilities, I highly doubted she would murder her over them.

His eyes continued boring into mine. "So, now you can see why I'm so interested in Anastasia's ... shall we say, emotional temperament, today."

I sighed. This wasn't a conversation I wanted to have, but I couldn't see a way out of it. "Well, unfortunately, you're going to discover that Anastasia was very stressed about the wedding and was taking out much of her frustration on the wedding planner. But I really don't think she would kill her."

"That remains to be seen," Wyle said, frantically scribbling in his notebook. "Was she upset with Jane today?"

I sighed again. "Yes. I overheard Anastasia yelling at Jane, basically telling her she sucked at her job. Again, I could totally see Anastasia firing her, but killing her is a step too far."

Wyle continued to focus on his notebook. "Do you know why Anastasia was so upset with Jane?"

"I don't know for sure, but I think it's because Bridget, James's ex-girlfriend, was here today."

That got his attention. He raised his head in surprise. "James, as in the groom?"

"Yep."

"His ex-girlfriend is *here*?"

"Yep. I even talked to her."

Wyle seemed to be at a loss. "Why? Who invited her?"

"That would be Anastasia's future mother-in-law."

Wyle's arms went slack. "Let me get this straight. The groom's mother invited his ex-girlfriend to his fiancé's wedding shower?"

"That's correct."

"Why?"

"I guess Bridget is an old family friend," I said. "She and James were basically raised together. And now that she's going into fashion, she's helping Blanche design her wedding wardrobe, which apparently necessitated Bridget's presence today ... so she could get a sense of the wedding brand and coordinate the clothes correctly."

Wyle's face was blank. "Do things like that often happen?"

I shrugged. "In wealthy circles, sure. They do a lot of strange things. Bridget claimed that Blanche had cleared it with Anastasia, who was fine with it."

"You think Bridget was lying? Or Blanche?"

I raised my hands, palms up. "I have no idea. It's certainly possible Blanche asked Anastasia, who wasn't able to come up with a polite way to say no to her future mother-in-law fast enough. So, she agreed out of a sense of obligation. But I can pretty much guarantee that Anastasia was not at all 'fine' with the arrangement." I placed air quotes around the word "fine."

"Do you think Anastasia is jealous of Bridget?" Wyle asked.

"I think you'd have to be awfully self-confident not to be," I said. "When you meet her, you'll understand what I mean. And Anastasia doesn't strike me as being nearly confident enough."

"Do you think she has reason to be jealous of Bridget?"

"Like, do I think James is cheating on Anastasia with Bridget? Again, I don't know, but he certainly sounded convincing to me, when he explained their relationship."

"What do you mean?"

"Well, recently James had lunch with Bridget, and ..."

Wyle held up his hand to stop me. "Hold on. He had lunch with her?"

"Yes. And his mother."

Wyle blinked at me. "The three of them had lunch."

"Yes."

"I'm almost afraid to ask why."

"Apparently, Blanche thought James might want to pick Bridget's brain about possible honeymoon trips."

Wyle shook his head as he made a note. "This is unbelievable."

"Anyway, James kept telling Anastasia he loved her ... that he wasn't interested in Bridget that way. They had grown up together, so he thought of her more as a sister than a potential mate. And like I said, he certainly seemed convincing."

"It doesn't sound like neither his mother nor Bridget is all that convinced," Wyle said drily.

"Yeah, it certainly does seem like Blanche would prefer Bridget as her daughter-in-law," I agreed. "Blanche keeps saying Bridget is just an old friend of the family, and it doesn't mean anything that she keeps turning up. But it's still quite ... odd."

"Do you think Bridget feels the same way as Blanche? That she would rather be the one marrying James?"

I held my hand up again. "I don't know. Maybe. When I asked her about it, she said pretty much the same thing that James had said. Although ..." I thought about how she had bumped into Anastasia, making her spill her tea all over. "I wouldn't rule out the possibility that Bridget wouldn't mind getting back together."

Wyle made a few more notes before frowning at them. "This would all feel more relevant if Anastasia was the one in the hospital instead of the wedding planner," he mused. "Other than Anastasia not being pleased with her performance, can you think of anyone else who didn't like Jane?"

"Honestly, she's kind of a mouse," I said. "From what I've seen, I find it hard to believe she would have done or said much of anything to inspire the kind of emotion needed to murder someone. I think people would be more likely to forget about her than want to kill her."

His lips quirked up again. "Well, someone disagrees."

"Maybe," I said, remembering Jane's penchant for champagne. "Do you know how she was poisoned? Was it something she ate or drank?"

"Not yet. We need to run more tests. Depending on what was used to poison her, it's possible it didn't even happen at the shower. Some poisons take longer to work."

"True," I said thoughtfully.

Wyle narrowed his eyes. "What? You know something, don't you?"

"I don't know if I know anything," I said. "It's just a thought."

He gave me an exasperated look. "Charlie, just spill it."

"You won't like it."

"I don't like anything about this case," he grumbled. "Whatever you say isn't going to change that."

I hid my smile. "Don't say I didn't warn you. I'm just wondering ... what if she wasn't the target?"

"What do you mean?"

I told him about how I caught Jane taking a swig of champagne when no one was looking. "After listening to Anastasia yell at Jane earlier, I have no doubt Jane was ready for a drink. And if she saw an unattended glass of champagne, it wouldn't surprise me if she quickly gulped it down, thinking no one would miss it, or if they did, that they would just get another glass. Of course, unfortunately for Jane, if that was where the poison came from, she simply chose the wrong glass."

"So, whoever was supposed to drink that champagne was the intended target, not Jane," Wyle surmised.

"Exactly."

"Do you have any idea whose champagne glass she would have drunk from?" Wyle asked.

"I can't even be sure she took someone else's glass," I said. "I didn't see her do it. I'm just saying, it's possible. And in my opinion, more likely than someone going out of his or her way to poison her."

Wyle closed his eyes and pinched the bridge of his nose. "What a nightmare. Now, everyone in that entire shower just turned into a potential suspect."

"One place you could start would be to see if anyone was handed a glass of champagne and put it down somewhere without drinking it," I said. "You're asking everyone questions anyway, right? Along with asking if anyone saw Jane eat or drink anything, maybe ask if anyone misplaced a champagne glass."

Wyle started scribbling notes. "Good idea. Anything else?"

"I don't think so," I said. "At least for the moment. And I probably need to get back to my bride-whispering duties, if you're done with me."

Wyle sighed. "I suppose it wouldn't matter if I told you not to get involved and to leave it to the professionals."

"It depends on what you mean by 'matter,'" I said. "If you mean it's something I make a mental note about, then sure, it matters."

Wyle gave me a look. "Just be careful," he said. "At this point, we have no idea what's even poisoned, much less who is responsible. Don't eat or drink anything."

"You don't have to worry about that," I said with a shiver.

Wyle's mouth was pressed in a grim line. "And if you're going to be involved, then make sure you tell me if you see or hear anything," he said.

"I know the drill," I said. "And don't worry, you'll be the first to know." I smiled sweetly at him as he shook his head. He didn't look convinced.

Chapter 6

"I told you there was something off with those quiches," Anastasia said to Mary Rose. "Didn't I tell you it tasted funny?"

"Honey, I don't think it was the quiche," Mary Rose said.

"Of course it was," Anastasia said. "What else would it be?"

I had found Anastasia, Mary Rose, and Dana huddled in a corner of the dining room. The rest of the guests were more or less split between the living room and the family room, while the cops apparently worked on making one of the spare bedrooms into a makeshift interrogation room to question them.

Anastasia glanced over at me. I was surprised at how composed she appeared, considering Jane's collapsing and ending up in the hospital were far worse than any other wedding issue she'd dealt with so far. But upon a closer look, I could see the tension around her lips and eyes. "Did you try the quiche?" she asked me.

"I didn't," I admitted.

"Definitely a good thing," she said, her mouth curled in disgust. "You could be in the hospital next to Jane right now."

"Jane ate the quiche?" My mind was whirling, and I wondered if I should excuse myself to tell Wyle, so he could test the quiches.

"We're not sure," Dana said, while at the same time, Anastasia answered, "She must have."

"Did you see her eat it, though?" I asked Anastasia.

Anastasia looked a little chagrined. "No. But, I told you, it tasted funny."

"Tasted funny how?" I asked. "Like it was poisoned?"

Anastasia's eyes widened in horror. "No! Like it was bad."

I was having trouble following her. "Bad? Like bad how?"

"Like food poisoning bad," Mary Rose said with a sigh.

I glanced between the two of them. "You think Jane is in the hospital over food poisoning?"

"Well, of course," Anastasia said impatiently. "What else?"

"Um …" I stammered, trying to decide if I should share with them what Wyle told me about the doctors suspecting poison. Ultimately, I decided it would be better coming from the cops.

As it turned out, I didn't need to say anything, after all. "Anastasia, dear, I don't think it was food poisoning," Dana said carefully.

"I agree. If it was, she would have been getting sick in the bathroom, not passing out in the middle of the yard," Mary Rose added.

"It could be a different type of food sickness," Anastasia insisted. "You're not a doctor, so you don't know."

"Maybe you're right," Mary Rose said, her voice resigned.

"Of course I'm right," Anastasia said. "Nothing else makes sense. She's a terrible wedding planner. Everything she touched was a disaster, including this! She chose the caterers, so of course they were dreadful. I'm just glad she was the only one to get sick from her incompetence."

"Anastasia," Mary Rose said, her face shocked. Even Dana looked stricken. "That's a terrible thing to say."

"But it's true," Anastasia said defiantly, lifting her chin up. Yet her face didn't look as confident as before. "She was horrible, and if anyone deserved to get sick, it was her."

A movement in the hallway caught my eye. I turned to see who was listening in, but whoever it was had already slipped past. An uneasy feeling lodged itself in the pit of my stomach. Anastasia's voice was loud enough to ensure that whoever was walking past had overheard her. Whether or not that person was paying attention was another matter, but if he or she was, and if Jane was really poisoned …

I didn't finish that train of thought. If Anastasia ended up having to explain herself, I would worry about it then.

Chapter 7

"Any news?" Pat asked me from the other end of the phone line the next morning.

"Not yet," I said.

"I'll be right over," she announced, and promptly hung up.

I put the receiver down, yawned, and headed into the kitchen to make a fresh pot of tea and plate some blueberry muffins I had baked a couple of days before.

It had been a long, exhausting day. I stuck around Dana's until dinner time, when the cops finally let most of the guests go. Dana told me I might as well head home as well, as they had already spoken to Anastasia, who was then taking a break and lying down in one of the bedrooms. As the afternoon had worn on, she had gone from complaining about Jane to growing more and more anxious that the wedding might be postponed. She tried calling James, but she couldn't reach him, so she found Blanche instead, despite the objections from Mary Rose, Dana, and myself.

Needless to say, Blanche was appalled by Anastasia worrying about her wedding when there was a young woman "fighting for her life" in the hospital. She told Anastasia they would discuss the wedding at a more appropriate time, which of course made Anastasia even more agitated. Finally, Dana convinced Anastasia to take one of her Xanax. I thought about mentioning that it wasn't a great idea to take someone else's prescription drugs, but Anastasia was such a twitchy mess at that point, I was fairly certain my warning would fall on deaf ears. I did, however, leave some tea with instructions for brewing a pot.

I hadn't been able to talk to Pat at all—she was excused earlier by the police and had Richard, her husband, come pick her up. If she hadn't called me, I would have reached out to her—I was eager to talk to her and ask her what she had seen at the shower, especially since she had apparently been closer to Jane when she collapsed.

Pat arrived a few minutes later, looking as exhausted and worn out as I felt. Even Tiki looked rough around the edges, with her crooked pink ribbons and wrinkled shirt. "What, you couldn't even dress Tiki in a new outfit?" I asked, handing Pat a cup of tea as she deposited Tiki on the floor.

Pat took a long drink. "Are you kidding? I was way too tired to do anything about her outfit last night."

"Yes, but it's morning."

Pat gave me a look as she reached for a muffin. "You're lucky *I'm* wearing a clean shirt. Tiki will be fine for one more day."

At the sound of her name, Tiki glanced up and then sat down, staring expectantly at the muffin in Pat's hand.

Pat sighed. "Oh, all right." She broke a piece off and tossed it to Tiki, who expertly caught it.

"So, you know I'm going to ask," I said.

Pat eyed me. "You want to know about Jane, don't you?"

"Well, you were right there when she collapsed," I said. "Not to mention you were the one who thought she was dead."

Pat dropped her gaze into her cup, her face paling slightly. "She really looked dead," she said softly. "I hope she makes it, but ..." she shook her head. "I'm no doctor, but she didn't look right to me."

"Do you think it was food poisoning?" I didn't think that was it at all, but I wondered if Anastasia's theory had gained any traction.

Pat gave me a sharp look. "Food poisoning? Is that what the doctors are saying?"

"It's what Anastasia is saying," I said.

"Why on Earth would she think that?" Pat asked. "Does she even know what food poisoning is?"

"Who knows," I said. "I think it's more that she doesn't want to think it's anything else. What do you think it was?"

"I thought she was having a seizure or a stroke. Something along those lines," Pat said. "But when the cops showed up and started questioning everyone, I assumed something else was going on."

"What did you see?"

Pat picked up her tea, cupping it in her hands for warmth. "Not a lot, I'm afraid. It wasn't like I was watching her, or anything. It was only when she started to go down that she caught my eye."

Crap. I had hoped Pat had seen something more. "So, you didn't see if she had eaten or drank anything?" I asked.

Pat shook her head. "Alas, no."

"Did you notice anything strange at all?"

"Other than her collapsing?"

My lips quirked up. "Yeah, other than that."

Pat sipped her tea. "Define 'strange.'"

"Well, was anyone near her, or watching her?"

"As it was a party, there were a lot of people around her, but I don't know if any of them were necessarily watching her," Pat said.

I figured that was a long shot. "Did you see if she had anything in her hands, or was carrying anything?"

"Other than the champagne glass that broke, I didn't see anything."

I sat up a little straighter. "Champagne glass?"

"Yeah. I accidentally knelt on it when I tried to help her. I cut my knee and everything." She stretched her leg out and showed me the Band-Aid.

"Did you see her drop it?"

"I'm not even sure it was hers," Pat said. "I figured she had been collecting dirty glasses and had dropped it when she collapsed, as it was next to her. But I suppose it's possible someone else dropped it."

In my mind's eye, I saw Jane in the kitchen, guzzling champagne. "If I had to bet, I would say it was Jane who dropped it."

"Really? What makes you so sure?"

"Because Jane wasn't averse to having a few sips of champagne at these events."

Pat's eyes widened. "You think she was drinking? But wasn't she working?"

"That didn't stop her before." I told Pat how I had caught her drinking at the cake tasting, following Anastasia's outbursts. "Anastasia was pretty upset with her yesterday, so I'd be more surprised if Jane *hadn't* snuck a few drinks again."

Pat continued to stare at me. I could almost see the wheels turning. "You think someone killed Jane by slipping poison in her champagne?"

"Possibly."

"Wow." Pat sat for a moment, mulling over the theory. "It's certainly possible she was poisoned," she continued. "I was thinking with the way the cops reacted, something like that was going on. But I was also assuming it was an accident, whatever it was. I mean, who would purposefully murder the wedding planner?"

"Maybe someone who doesn't want the wedding to happen," I said, seeing Bridget in my mind's eye, and how she had "accidentally" shoved Anastasia.

"Yeah, but you can always hire another wedding planner," Pat said. "So it would only be a temporary solution."

"That might be enough," I said, thinking about all the ways Bridget was finding to spend time with James. "It's possible even a short delay could cause one of the engaged to rethink things."

"You honestly think one of them is going to have second thoughts?" Pat asked.

I shrugged. "It's less about me and more about what someone else is thinking. For instance, perhaps an ex-girlfriend isn't so happy about being an ex, and also thinks that the future groom is still in love with her. In that case, she might think he just needs a few nudges to be reminded of it."

Pat stared at me. "You think Bridget poisoned the wedding planner?"

"I have no idea. But I think it's something to take a closer look at."

Pat kept staring at me. "You really think Bridget is a murderer?"

"I didn't say *that*," I said. "First of all, Jane isn't dead. At least as far as I know. So there's no murder. But it's very possible that there was never supposed to *be* a murder. Maybe Bridget was just trying to make Jane sick, so Jane would quit, which would force Anastasia to delay the wedding … thus giving Bridget time to use her wiles to woo James back."

"Hmm." Pat took another bite of her muffin. "Interesting theory," she said while chewing. "Most murders are over love or money, although as you pointed out, it's not a murder yet."

"Depending on what Bridget used to poison Jane, it could be construed as an attempted murder, though," I said as the phone rang.

"What we really need to know is what exactly caused Jane to collapse," Pat said as I headed over to the phone. "Maybe Wyle is calling to tell us that."

"Ha," I said, picking up the phone.

"Oh, thank goodness. Charlie, you're there."

"Dana?" I asked. I could barely recognize her voice. "Is there news? Do you know how Jane is doing?"

"Not good." Dana's voice was breathless, as if she had been running and paused to call me. "Not good at all. She's dead."

"Dead?" At the table, Pat stopped chewing and got up to move closer to the phone. "Oh no. That's horrible."

"That's not the worst of it," Dana said. "I mean … that sounded really bad. I know, it's terrible that she's dead, but …" There was a garbled sound, and despite not understanding what I was hearing, I was starting to get a terrible feeling.

"Dana? Are you still there? What's worse?"

"It's Anastasia," Dana said, and I suddenly realized Dana was crying. "She's been arrested for Jane's murder!"

Chapter 8

Pat and I found Dana and Mary Rose in the lobby of the police station. They were huddled together on the bright-orange, hard-plastic chairs, but both were on their feet as soon as they saw me. "Thank goodness you're here," Dana said, her voice filled with relief. I did a double take, as I almost didn't recognize her. She hadn't done her hair and makeup yet, and I was a little shocked at how much younger she looked without it. "You have to get Anastasia out of there."

"You're our only hope," Mary Rose pleaded. Along with no makeup, her hair was a tangled mess, like she had just gotten up and hadn't even run a brush through it. Her eyes were red and puffy, too, making it clear she had been crying. "How could they think Anastasia could do anything like this? She doesn't even kill spiders! She could never kill another human being. You have to get her out of there. She doesn't belong in prison."

"Did you call a lawyer?" I asked, really hoping I wasn't going to have to explain to Dana that along with not being any sort of doctor, I also wasn't an attorney.

"Yes, yes," Dana said, flapping her hands. "He's already gotten an emergency bail hearing with a judge today."

That was a relief. At least Dana didn't expect me to argue for bail in front of a judge. "Well, that's good."

"Yes, but bail isn't enough," Dana said. "We need to get these charges dropped."

"I agree, that would be ideal," I said cautiously. "But you do know that's not really under my control."

"Oh, for heaven's sake." Dana flapped her hands again, her voice exasperated. "Charlie, everyone knows you're the one who solves the murders around here. You have to take Anastasia's case! You know she didn't do it!"

I cringed slightly, glancing around to see if anyone had overheard. I didn't think the other officers would take too kindly to my getting the credit for doing their jobs. "Dana, that's not exactly true ..."

"Of course it is," Dana said. "You're being too modest. As usual."

"You *are* pretty modest," Pat said.

I slapped Pat on the shoulder. "That's not the point," I admonished. "We need to work with the cops ..."

"We'll pay you, of course," Dana interrupted.

"Yes, of course," Mary Rose chimed in. "Whatever you want."

"It's not the money," I said. "I just prefer to work with the cops and not against them."

"Do whatever you need to do," Dana said. "I don't care how you do it. Just get the charges dropped. Anastasia didn't do this. You know she's innocent."

"I'll do my best," I said, glancing around again, this time hoping to maybe catch a glimpse of Wyle. I had a lot of questions that likely only he could answer.

"Does that mean you'll help us?" Mary Rose asked.

"Yes," I said. "I'll try."

Dana clapped her hands. "Oh! I knew you'd come through!"

"No promises, though," I said. "I'll do what I can, but that doesn't mean I'll be successful."

Dana was visibly relieved. "Yes, yes. Whatever. I know you'll find the truth. I have complete confidence in you."

"Like that's not a ton of pressure," Pat said in a low voice. I nudged her again, not wanting Dana to overhear, but it didn't matter, as Dana wasn't paying any attention.

"As soon as we get the bail straightened out, you'll need to talk to Anastasia," Dana insisted. "We can bring her back to my house. That might be easiest. And then, you'll have to tell us who you want to interview next."

"Yes," Mary Rose said. "Whatever you need, just tell us. We'll do anything."

I held up a hand, trying to slow the flow of words. "Let's start with some background info. Do you know what exactly happened to Jane? When she died or what killed her?"

"No, we don't know anything," Dana said.

"The first we heard that Jane was dead was when Anastasia called me from the police station, telling me she had been arrested," Mary Rose said.

"Did Anastasia give you any details?"

"No, she was too hysterical," Mary Rose said. "She was terrified of spending any time in jail, so the first thing I had to do was find a lawyer to get her out on bail."

"What about when the cops questioned you? Did they ask you anything that seemed out of place?" I asked.

"All of the questions were out of place," Dana grumbled. "They kept asking about Anastasia's relationship with Jane. I kept telling them Anastasia had nothing to do with it, and they needed to do more investigating, but they wouldn't listen."

"Did they ask anything about poisons? Or plants or herbs?" I asked, still hoping to get a clue as to what killed Jane.

"No, nothing like that," Dana said. "But they did take a bunch of stuff. Bagged it all up, asked me if it was mine."

"Like what?"

"Oh, you know. A bunch of cleaning products. Antifreeze. Oh, what else?" Dana asked, looking at Mary Rose.

"Didn't they find that old rat poison in the back of the garage?" Mary Rose asked.

"Oh, yes. That. And insecticide. And all my prescription drugs. Ugh. I need to get those back, too," Dana said.

That sounded more like a fishing expedition than anyone having a clear idea of what precisely killed Jane. I was going to ask another question when I spotted Wyle near the back of the station. He was talking to another officer and didn't see me. "Hold on ... I'll be right back," I said, quickly darting toward him, hoping if I moved fast, no one would stop me.

It almost worked. No one else noticed me, but I was about halfway to Wyle when he glanced over and saw me. I could almost see him sigh.

He said something to the officer and came toward me. "I shouldn't be surprised you're here," he said.

"Dana called me," I said briskly.

At that, he did sigh. "Of course she did."

"Why do you think it was Anastasia?" I asked.

"Evidence," Wyle said. "Maybe you've heard of it?"

"Very funny," I said. "What evidence?"

"Well, to start, she had access to the drugs that killed Jane."

"Drugs?" I was surprised. "I thought Jane was poisoned."

"No, it turns out it was a prescription drug overdose," Wyle said.

My mind flashed back to what Dana said about the cops raiding her medicine cabinet. "Was it one of Dana's prescriptions?"

He shot me a hard look. "How did you know?"

"Lucky guess," I said. "Which drug?"

"One I hadn't heard of before," he said. "It's apparently an anti-anxiety medication."

I gave him a curious look. "That you've never heard of?"

"You find that so surprising?" He countered. "I'm a cop, not a pharmacist."

"Well, yes," I said. "I just assumed you've had dealings with other people overdosing on prescription drugs, so you would be familiar with most of them."

"True," Wyle said, his expression thoughtful. "But in this case, it's really new. The M.E. hadn't heard of it, either, and had to do some research. He thought it might even still be experimental, but that doesn't seem right."

I was surprised Dana had been prescribed something that new. "If it was, how would Anastasia know it would kill Jane?"

"Lucky guess," Wyle said.

"Seriously? That's what you're going with?"

Wyle's lips quirked up. "The label does say to avoid mixing it with alcohol, so we're guessing that's where Anastasia got the idea. But we're still investigating."

"Seems like a bit of a reach, don't you think?"

"Maybe, but on the other hand, it sure seems like it would have had to come from Dana's medicine cabinet. There's not a lot of people in this town who would have access to that specific drug."

"What about Dana?"

He looked at me in surprise. "You think Dana killed Jane?"

"Of course not. Just like I don't think Anastasia killed her. But Dana had access to the drugs just as much as Anastasia did, so why aren't you investigating her?"

"Well, Dana doesn't have a motive, for one," Wyle said.

"And Anastasia does?"

"We have multiple witnesses, including Anastasia herself, who claim that she didn't like Jane," Wyle said. "We also have multiple witnesses saying Anastasia was acting erratic. Crazy, even. No one is saying that about Dana."

"That doesn't mean Anastasia did it," I said, even as my stomach sank. Wyle's case against her was more compelling than I'd realized. "Anyone who was in Dana's house the day of the shower had access to Dana's medicine cabinet."

Wyle's expression was skeptical. "You really want me to believe that someone else at the shower decided to rifle through Dana's medicine cabinet, hoping to find a drug they could use to kill the wedding planner?"

Argh. When he put it like that, it did sound out there. "Okay, so what if it wasn't murder? What if it was an accident?"

Wyle raised an eyebrow. "An accident? Sure, one of Dana's prescription drugs ended up in something Jane ate or drank by accident. Happens all the time."

I ignored his sarcastic tone. "I was thinking it might have been Jane herself."

"Jane? You think she tried to commit suicide?"

"No, I think she might have been rifling through Dana's medicine cabinet looking for something stronger than alcohol,"

I said. The image of Anastasia yelling at Jane and the stressed look on Jane's face made me wonder if Anastasia pushed Jane a little too hard, and Jane decided champagne alone wasn't going to cut it. "Jane had been in Dana's house multiple times. It's possible she had snooped before and knew there were anti-anxiety drugs in the medicine cabinet, and after the dressing down she got from Anastasia, decided it was time to see if a prescription drug worked better than alcohol."

"Dana didn't think Jane had ever been in that medicine cabinet," Wyle said,

"That doesn't mean she hadn't," I said. "We already know Jane was sneaking champagne. Is it that much of a stretch to think she might have been poking around for something stronger?"

Wyle didn't immediately answer, but his face was thoughtful as he pulled his notebook out of his pocket.

"Honestly, Jane accidentally overdosing makes the most sense," I argued, sensing I might have found an opening. "She would have been drinking for sure. It seems pretty clear that she was a heavy drinker, if not an alcoholic. And it's possible she didn't realize the dangers of mixing drugs and booze, even with the warning on the label."

"Or, she disregarded it. Didn't think it was important," Wyle said, scribbling a note. "We'll look into it."

"Does that mean you'll drop the charges against Anastasia?" I asked, mentally crossing my fingers. Could it be that easy?

Wyle gave me a look as he put the notebook away. "We'll look into it," he repeated.

I sighed. So much for it being that easy.

He was watching me closely. "That also means you don't need to be involved," he said. "Right?"

"Of course," I said, my voice sweet.

He crossed his arms. "Charlie," he said, his tone warning. "I know Anastasia is your client, but that doesn't mean you should be poking around in this. It could be dangerous. If Anastasia didn't do it, we'll get to the bottom of it. Okay?"

"I hope you do get to the bottom of it," I said before glancing at the clock on the wall. "Oh, goodness me. Look at the time. I have to go."

"Charlie," Wyle said. "I'm serious. The chances of this being an accident are slim, which means there's a killer running around out there."

"But, according to you, it's Anastasia," I said. "And if I'm looking into proving Anastasia's innocence, why would she do anything to hurt me?"

"And if it's not Anastasia?" Wyle asked, his eyes narrowing. "Now you have a killer who thinks they've gotten away with it, and when you start poking around, you open yourself up to being a target."

"I guess we both better hope you catch whoever it is first," I said. I flashed him a smile and offered a quick wave as I turned to head back to Dana.

Wyle pressed his hands against his temple. "Charlie, I swear, you're going to be the death of me."

Chapter 9

Dana and Mary Rose weren't in the police station lobby. The desk clerk informed me that Anastasia had been granted bail, and Dana and Mary Rose had gone to take care of it. Dana had also left me a note requesting I go straight to Dana's house, as Anastasia would definitely be requiring my services. She also asked me to bring lots and lots of tea.

I headed home to fetch my bag of teas before going to Dana's, a little bemused at the specific instructions. Was I supposed to stand on the stoop until Dana arrived home with Anastasia and Mary Rose? As it turned out, Dana had called her husband at work, asking him to come home to let me in, which he did, although it seemed clear he was doing it to stay out of the drama as much as possible.

I busied myself making tea, and when they still didn't arrive, decided to bake a batch of Snicker Doodle cookies while I waited. With the day those three were having, sugar was in order.

I was just taking them out of the oven when they arrived. "Oh, that smells heavenly," Dana exclaimed, coming into the kitchen. "You made cookies? You didn't have to do that."

"I figured you all had a big shock today," I said, transferring them onto a cooling rack. "Sugar is always helpful with shock."

"I shouldn't," Dana mused, staring longingly at one of the cookies. "It will ruin my diet."

"Calories don't count on days when your niece gets arrested for murder," I said.

Dana cocked her head, her face thoughtful. "Good point," she said. "They probably don't count when it's your daughter, either."

"Absolutely not," I said. "Nor if you yourself are arrested."

Dana nodded and picked up a cookie, blowing on it, as it was still hot. "Anastasia and Mary Rose will be thrilled. I'm sure they'll definitely be up for some of these when they come down."

"Come down?"

Dana nodded as she took a bite. "She's in the shower," she said around a mouthful of cookie. "Said she had to wash the jail stink off of her. But she knows you're here and shouldn't be too long. Mary Rose is with her."

"I don't blame her for wanting a shower," I said, although I privately doubted it not taking long. Anastasia would likely take her own sweet time. I didn't think that was a bad thing, though, as it would give me a chance to ask Dana a few questions. "So, did you hear anything more about how Jane died?"

"No!" Dana said, her voice exasperated. "No one is telling us anything. The lawyer said he needs time to review what the prosecutor sent over, and then he'll talk to us, but with what we're paying him, he should be more on the ball."

"Well, it was a little last minute," I said. "He probably had other things going on today."

Dana flapped her hand at me. "Yes, that was his excuse. He had to be back in court or something." She rolled her eyes. "Anyway, I guess I should be grateful he was able to get Anastasia out on bail so quickly." She didn't sound particularly grateful, but I decided to ignore that. "I still don't understand why she was even arrested. The police can't possibly think she had anything to do with Jane's death."

"Well, it appears Jane overdosed on one of your prescription drugs," I said.

"I'm sure it wasn't one of MY prescriptions," Dana said firmly. "All those drugs were in my bathroom, which is connected to my bedroom. There's no reason for anyone to have gone in there."

"The M.E. seemed pretty convinced it was one of yours," I said.

"How would he know?" she asked, her voice indignant. "Was my name on the pills?"

"Well, no," I said.

"Exactly," Dana said smugly. "Lots of people have the same prescription drugs I do. It's just a coincidence, if one of them used the same one I have."

"That may be true for some of them," I said. "But at least one is so new, the M.E. didn't even know what it was."

Dana looked surprised. "Which one is that?"

"The anti-anxiety one."

Dana frowned. "I have a couple of different types for anxiety. Do you know which one it was?"

"You have more than one anti-anxiety medicine?" I tried to conceal my surprise and keep my question more neutral, but I suspected I failed miserably.

Dana's expression was defensive. "Anxiety is a huge problem," she said. "Millions of Americans suffer from it."

"I'm sure," I said quickly, but Dana kept talking.

"There's no shame in getting the help you need," she said. "It's really quite debilitating."

"Of course," I said. "I meant no offense. I was just surprised you had more than one prescription."

"Well, sometimes the first one doesn't work," she said, her body stiff. "Sometimes, you have to try a few."

I hadn't considered that Dana might have needed to try different medications in order to find one that was right for her, but now that she said it, I wondered if that was why she had something new and experimental in her medicine cabinet. "I'm really sorry," I said. "I didn't mean to offend you."

Almost immediately, her shoulders sagged, and her body seemed to go limp. "No, it's me, not you," she said, uncharacteristically raking a hand through her hair and leaving it more tangled and mussed than before. "I'm completely out of sorts right now. Everything happened so fast, I can't get my head around it. How did we get here? How could anyone think my darling Anastasia would have anything to do with Jane's death? She could lose everything over this."

I reached over to squeeze her arm. "I know. It's tough. It's hard to believe we were all at Anastasia's shower just yesterday."

Dana's expression was full of gratitude as she met my eyes. "I know! I knew you'd understand. It's just crazy how it all unfolded. I can't tell you how relieved we all are that you're here to sort it out. I knew you'd understand. And ..." her eyes darted to the side of me as her voice trailed off. "Anastasia! Love, you didn't need to come in here. We could have brought anything you needed out to you."

I turned around to see Anastasia, still damp, wearing a white terrycloth towel. Her hair hung in wet curls around her shoulders, and her face was scrubbed clean of makeup. She looked young—way too young to be engaged to be married.

"It's okay, Aunt Dana," Anastasia said, her voice tired. "I thought I heard Charlie's voice."

"I'm making you some tea, and there are fresh-baked cookies here," I said.

She nodded, her expression listless as she stared at the counter, but she didn't move to take anything. "I guess I could have a cookie. It's not like I have to fit into a wedding dress anymore."

"Don't you think like that," Dana said, pushing the cookies closer to her. "James loves you. You know this. Heavens, everyone knows it, just by looking at the boy. Once Charlie sorts this out, you'll be walking down the aisle exactly as planned. In the meantime, a cookie or two won't hurt."

"No, a cookie isn't going to make a bit of difference," Mary Rose said. She had come in behind Anastasia, and unlike her daughter, she looked like she was aging by the moment. Her face was flushed, likely from the heat of the shower, which only emphasized the folds and wrinkles on her skin. She picked up a cookie to hand to Anastasia, who took it limply, letting it fall to the counter. Mary Rose gave her a distressed look. "Sweetie, you should really eat something."

"Later," Anastasia said, her voice devoid of emotion. "I'm not hungry."

"I'm not surprised," I quickly interjected, as I could see both Dana and Mary Rose opening their mouths to protest. "Why don't you try a little tea?" I scooted the mug across the counter toward her. "You're probably still in shock, with everything that happened. The tea should calm your stomach down."

She picked up the tea dutifully but didn't take a sip. Instead, she just stared into the cup. "I knew I never should have hired her," she said, her voice mournful.

Next to me, I saw Mary Rose and Dana eye each other nervously. "Who are you talking about?" Dana asked.

"Jane," Anastasia said, raising her head. "I knew she was trouble from the moment I laid eyes on her."

Dana blanched. "Anastasia, you don't mean that," she said as Mary Rose pressed a hand against her mouth, her eyes round with shock. "Jane tried her best," Dana continued. "It's not her fault she was in over her head."

"And besides, we shouldn't speak ill of the dead," Mary Rose added.

"Why not?" Anastasia asked. Now that I was closer, I could see that her eyes were red-rimmed and her face blotchy, as if all she had done in the shower was cry. Not that I blamed her. "Just because she's dead doesn't change the fact that she was a horrible wedding planner."

"Anastasia!" Both women gasped at the same time. "You don't mean that," Dana continued, her expression horrified as she glanced at me. "She doesn't know what she's saying," she said.

Anastasia whirled around, still holding the mug of tea as some of it sloshed over the side. "I know exactly what I'm saying," she said, waving one of her arms. "Jane was supposed to be on my side! She was supposed to be planning my perfect, dream wedding! Instead, she hires a caterer who accidentally kills her with food poisoning, and somehow, it's all my fault?"

"Jane didn't die from food poisoning," I said before Dana could admonish Anastasia again. I put a hand on Dana's arm, gently squeezing.

Anastasia shot me a peculiar look. "Well, of course she did. What other explanation is there?"

I shook my head. "She died from an overdose of a prescription drug."

Anastasia's jaw dropped. "She overdosed herself? And *that's* my fault?" Her voice started to climb in righteous anger. "Of all the nerve ..."

"It wasn't her prescription," I interrupted before Anastasia could work herself into a rage.

"Well, whose was it?" Anastasia demanded.

"We don't know," Dana answered gently.

Anastasia threw her hands up in the air. "So, Jane is stealing other people's prescription drugs, and I'm the one they're blaming?"

"It's true there's a lot we don't know," I said. "But it appears Jane took some sort of new anti-anxiety medicine. It's possible she was drinking, as well, and if she was, the combination could have been lethal."

"Again," Anastasia said. "How is any of that my fault?"

I eyed Dana, who was starting to look nervous again. Anastasia saw us exchange a look. "What?" she demanded.

Dana cleared her throat as she reached up with one slender hand to fiddle with the collar of her shirt. "It appears to have been one of my prescription drugs," she said. "Although there's still no direct evidence of that."

Anastasia stared at Dana. "Are you saying Jane snuck into your bathroom to steal one of your prescriptions? That thief!"

"We don't know if that's what happened," I said. "It's certainly possible that was the case, but it's also possible someone slipped her the drugs."

Anastasia shifted her eyes to me. "What? That's what the cops think happened? That I poisoned Jane with my aunt's prescription drugs?"

I met her gaze. "Yes, that's exactly what they think," I said, my voice firm. "And quite honestly, your attitude isn't helping anything."

Her eyes widened. "My ... my attitude?" Next to me, I could see Dana close her eyes.

"Yes. Blaming Jane isn't going to help."

"But ... but ..." Anastasia stuttered. "I'm being charged with murder!"

"I know," I said, softening my voice. "And do you understand why?"

"Because the cops are idiots?"

"No, because you're acting like a spoiled brat."

Silence. Anastasia sucked in her breath and brought both hands to her face, as if I had slapped her. "What ... how can you say that to me?"

"I'm not trying to be mean," I said. "Believe it or not, I'm trying to help. You're your own worst enemy right now. Part of the reason the cops have zeroed in on you is because you're the only one with a motive for killing her."

Anastasia's mouth worked. "I don't ... how can you say that? Just because I think she's incompetent ..."

"Yes," I interrupted. "All you've been doing is going on and on about how much you dislike Jane. Of course the cops are going to think you had something to do with it, especially since it appears you had access to the drugs that killed her."

Anastasia gaped at me as the blood drained from her face. Her eyes were wide, and for a moment, I thought I might have gone too far.

Dana might have been thinking the same, because she swept in then, putting an arm around her niece. "Are you okay? Maybe you should sit down for a moment."

Anastasia didn't move. "Do you think I'm acting like a spoiled brat?" she asked Dana.

Dana puckered her mouth, like she had just eaten a lemon. "You've been really stressed," she said. "Planning a wedding is always difficult."

Anastasia narrowed her eyes. "You're not answering the question."

Dana sighed. "It would help if you weren't so hard on Jane," she said. "Especially as she's dead, and the police think it's murder. It's not a good look. And you know how important it is to keep up appearances."

Anastasia bit her lip. "I really screwed up, didn't I?"

"Maybe not," I said. "You haven't been convicted of anything yet. There's still time to figure out what really happened."

Anastasia didn't appear to be listening. "I messed everything up," she said, her eyes beginning to fill with tears. "I've lost James, and I'm probably going to jail for something I didn't do. How did this happen?"

"Oh sweetie," Dana said, squeezing her from one side as Mary Rose bustled over and hugged her from the other. "You can't think like that. The worst thing you can do is give into despair."

"James loves you," Mary Rose said. "You haven't lost him. You just have to have faith."

Anastasia was openly crying then, still holding her untouched mug in one hand as tea continued sloshing over the sides and onto the floor. *Good thing I didn't put any sugar in it*, I thought, eying the growing puddle on the floor. Normally, under these kinds of circumstances, I would have, but this time, I had been relying on her eating a cookie, instead.

"Mom, you don't understand," Anastasia said, barely able to speak, she was crying so hard. "He's not going to wait for me if I go to jail."

"Honey, that's not going to happen," Dana said firmly. "Remember, we have Charlie on our side. She's the best detective in Wisconsin. Maybe even the entire Midwest."

"I don't know if I would go that far," I said quickly. Geez, talk about setting unrealistic expectations. "I'm not a detective, and even if I were, I wouldn't be the best in Redemption. Wyle is pretty good."

"Oh, Wyle." Dana rolled her eyes, her tone disgusted. "If Wyle had half a brain, he would realize there is no possible way my Anastasia could have anything to do with Jane's death."

"He's just following the evidence," I started to say, but Dana glared at me with such intensity, I amended my words. "It's true I've been pretty successful solving cases, as well, and I'm going to do everything in my power to find out what really happened."

"See?" Dana said triumphantly to Anastasia, who was still crying so hard, I wasn't sure she had followed the conversation. Tears and snot streaked her face, and I wondered if I should take her mug and hand her a box of tissues, instead. "I told you, you're in good hands." Anastasia continued to cry. As difficult as she was, it was impossible to be in that kitchen and not feel sorry for her. Just a couple of days before, she was on top of the world, getting ready to marry the love of her life, a surgeon-in-training who was also an heir to one of the richest families in southern Wisconsin. And now, her entire life had been shattered.

Yes, she had been a total pain in the you-know-what, but she was also young and probably a little full of herself when it came to who she was marrying. Maybe she deserved to be taken down a peg or two, but this was pretty intense.

Dana and Mary Rose kept murmuring to Anastasia to stop crying ... that it would all be okay. Their expressions were helpless as they stared at each other above her head. I couldn't stand it anymore and finally decided someone had to take charge.

"Anastasia, why don't you sit down, and I'll get you some fresh tea?" I suggested, reaching out to remove the cup from her limp hand. Dana shot me a grateful look. "You're in shock," I said, keeping my voice brisk. "Which is completely understandable, under the circumstances. Go on ... sit at the table." I gently pushed her to get her feet moving. As Mary Rose and Dana led her to a chair, I snatched a tissue box that was sitting under the wall phone and shoved it in Dana's hand.

I quickly made another cup, this time adding a healthy dollop of sugar. I also snuck a peek in the liquor cupboard and found an open bottle of brandy, and added a shot of that in the cup, as well.

Anastasia was still gasping and hiccupping, but by the time I had finished preparing her mug, the tears had slowed. I handed it to her free hand, as the other held a crumbled wet tissue she was using to scrub at her face. "Drink this," I said firmly. "You'll feel better."

She nodded and took a gulp, making a face as she forced herself to swallow. "Ugh. Is that ... is that alcohol?"

"Yes," I said. "It will help with the shock, too."

Her expression was unconvinced, but she took another longer drink. By the time she set her mug down, her hands had stopped trembling and her breathing steadied.

"See? Charlie makes everything better," Dana said as she patted Anastasia's arm. "You just leave everything up to her, and she'll get you out of this mess in no time."

"Uh ..." I started.

"So, I won't go to jail?" Anastasia asked in a small voice.

"Heavens, of course not," Dana said. "You don't need to worry that pretty head of yours at all. Charlie is going to get all of this sorted out."

"Um, Dana ..." I tried to say.

"That's a relief," Anastasia said, twisting the wet tissue in her hand. "Thank you, Charlie."

"Don't thank me yet," I said. "I haven't done anything ..."

"Oh, there she goes again, being modest," Dana said.

I briefly closed my eyes. I was going to have to speak to Dana about setting such expectations.

Anastasia was still twisting the wet clump of tissues, which was dissolving in her hands and showering the table with damp flakes. Dana gave her a worried look. "Have some more tea," she said, pushing the mug closer. "Something else is still bothering you. What is it?"

She obediently took another sip. "It's James," she said, licking her lips. "What if Charlie finds out what really happened, but he still doesn't want me?" Her face twisted up like she was going to cry again. Dana's expression was alarmed as she yanked more tissues out of the box.

"Sweetie, that is absolutely not going to happen. Don't cry. James adores you. Of course he still wants to marry you."

"But ... but ..." Anastasia stuttered as she grabbed the tissues and dabbed at her eyes. "He doesn't want to talk to me now."

"Well, he's probably just busy ..." Dana started to say, but I jumped in, putting a hand out to stop her from talking.

"Wait. What did you say?" I asked.

"He won't talk to me."

"How do you know?"

"Because I tried calling him," she said.

"When?"

"Before my shower," she said, her eyes filling with tears again. "But his mother answered and said he didn't want to talk to me."

I leaned forward. "Anastasia," I said, my voice urgent. "You can't talk to him."

Anastasia stared at me, so surprised, the tears seemed to instantly run out. "Why? He's my fiancé."

"Because this is a murder investigation," I said. "We don't know what he knows or whether he's involved."

All three of the women were staring at me with matching horrified expressions, and then, they all started talking at once. "You can't possibly think James had anything to do with it," Mary Rose said. "He's a Duckworth, for goodness said. What are you thinking?" Dana exclaimed. "James wouldn't kill anyone, much less Jane," Anastasia insisted.

I held up my hand again to get them to stop. "I didn't say James had anything to do with it," I said. "But that doesn't mean he isn't involved. It's possible the killer and James are connected somehow, even if James doesn't know it. James could say something to the killer that inadvertently tips him or her off."

Anastasia's mouth dropped open. "You think James might be in danger?"

"I didn't say that, either," I said quickly. "Nor do I necessary think it. But we need to be careful, is all ... at least until we know what's going on."

Dana still looked miffed. "James couldn't possibly know the killer," she said. "He's a Duckworth."

"Yes, well, you did say that Blanche was the one who recommended Jane, didn't you?" I asked. "Which means it's possible James knows more than you think."

Dana stared at me, her face suddenly brightening. "Of course. How could I forget? Charlie, you're a genius. See, she's going to solve this case in no time."

"Wait, I'm not ..." I started to say, but Dana cut me off.

"You need to go see Blanche right away and learn everything you can about Jane," Dana said. "Find out who recommended her, and see if you can dig into Jane's history. If Jane didn't do this to herself, accidentally of course," she hurriedly added, "then I'm sure someone in her past is the culprit."

"Can you also give James a message?" Anastasia asked, her voice hopeless. "Can you tell him I miss him?"

"Of course, if I see him," I said. "And I'm happy to talk with Blanche. But what excuse should I give her? There's no reason for me to go seek her out."

Dana waved her hand at me. "Oh, you'll figure something out. I have total confidence in you. Maybe bring Pat. It seemed like Blanche really liked that toy poodle of hers."

Chapter 10

"Such a dreadful thing to have happened," Blanche said as she sipped her tea and slipped Tiki a dog biscuit. "I still can't believe it."

"It's terrible," Pat agreed, sitting next to Blanche on the stiff, formal couch covered with a dusky, rose-colored, Damask brocade fabric. I was across from them on one of two matching chairs. A rose-colored rug covered the hardwood floor, and a vase of pale, pink roses accented the glass and gold coffee table. The room even smelled like roses—well, more like rose-scented air freshener.

As it turned out, we didn't need much of an excuse to visit Blanche. She was eager to invite Pat and me over for tea. She had been wanting to try more of my blends, she said, and was always happy to see little Tiki.

But it was clear that what she really wanted was gossip.

"Although, it IS Redemption we're talking about," Pat continued. Her tone was bland, as if she were having a run-of-the-mill dull conversation, but there was a wicked gleam in her eyes that made my heart sink. Sometimes, Pat enjoyed stirring the pot. "Strange things do happen here a lot."

Blanche pursed her lips in a disapproving manner. She was dressed in a similar, understated-yet-elegant outfit as the last times I'd seen her—ivory silk blouse, pearls, and pressed black trousers. Maybe that was what she always wore, I considered. "That's true. I don't know how you're able to stand to live there."

"Well, Redemption doesn't always give us a choice," Pat said. "Sometimes, we just have to make do."

Along with a lot of peculiar happenings in Redemption, Wisconsin, many of the townspeople believed that the town itself decided who stays and who goes. I was a bit skeptical of the notion, myself—after all, a town making decisions seemed pretty impossible. But I also couldn't explain the odd series of events that caused me to find myself living there.

Of course, there were a lot of things about Redemption I couldn't explain. It was a strange and haunted town, even as far back as 1888, when all the adults disappeared seemingly out of the blue, leaving only the children. No one knew what happened to the adults—even the children claimed they had no idea. They insisted the adults were there when they went to bed, but when they woke up, every single one of them was gone. Since then, many strange happenings, disappearances, and of course, murders, plagued the town.

"I suppose," Blanche said, but her expression was one of disbelief. "Have you spoken to Anastasia yet?"

Pat shook her head and gestured toward me. "Charlie has."

Blanche turned to me, her face lighting up with the promise of gossip. "Poor dear. How is she doing?"

"About as well as can be expected," I said.

Blanche shook her head sadly. "I can only imagine. I was so shocked when I heard the news about Jane. Such a tragedy. Her whole life ahead of her. It's always worse the younger they are, don't you think?"

"No question," I said, sipping my tea out of a delicate white-and-gold china cup that looked much better than the tea inside tasted. Although I had brought some of mine with me, Blanche had used something else. "It must have been dreadful for you, as well."

Blanche cocked her head, her little birdlike eyes gleaming at me. "What do you mean?"

"Well, you must have known Jane fairly well, right?" I asked. "Since you recommended Anastasia hire her."

"Oh." Blanche carefully reached over to replace her cup on the coffee table. "I see what you mean. While yes, I was the one who referred Jane to Anastasia, I didn't actually *know* her. She had been recommended to me by the Wilsons. I think Jane was their middle son's wedding planner. Anyway, when Anastasia first asked about one, I obviously didn't have an answer for her. It's not like I've planned a wedding recently. James is an only child, and this will be his first wedding. But I wanted to establish a good relationship with who I thought was my soon-to-be daughter-in-law, so I asked around and found Jane. If I had any idea what would eventually happen ..." she shook her head again.

It wasn't lost on me that she spoke of Anastasia being her new daughter-in-law in the past tense. "I see. I guess I was under the impression you had more of a relationship with her."

"No, not really. I just saw her at the various wedding outings. Much like you."

"So, you wouldn't have known if anyone was angry with her or wanted her dead for some reason."

Blanche's perfectly made-up eyes went wide, and she clutched at her pearls with a manicured hand. "I should say not! What do you take me for? If I had known someone was that upset with her, I never would have recommended her to Anastasia."

Fair point. "Did you have a chance to talk to the Wilsons about her? Maybe they could shed some light on her background or past. That might prove useful."

Blanche shook her head. "When I called them, they were shocked and horrified, of course, but they weren't aware of anyone wanting to harm Jane, either. They thought Jane had been perfectly pleasant. A little on the quiet side, but she got the job done and did it with very little fuss and no drama." Blanche sighed. "Quite honestly, I don't understand why Anastasia had so much trouble with her. My best guess is that it was a simple personality clash. Not everyone is suited for everyone."

"That is true," I agreed. "So, do you have a theory as to what happened to Jane?"

She reached out for her tea, taking a moment to mentally compose her answer. "Well, the police certainly think it was Anastasia," she said. "It's been my understanding that when the police are zeroing in on someone, they probably have reason to. So, while I can't believe Anastasia had anything to do with that poor girl's death, I really don't know what to think."

I took another sip of tea, nodding, but inside, I was thinking what a lukewarm defense that was of the woman her son wanted to marry. Maybe Anastasia had dodged a bullet, after all.

The front door slammed, and footsteps sounded on the foyer. My back was to the hallway, so I didn't see who came in, but I did see Blanche's face break into a smile. "James! How lovely to see you! And I see you brought Bridget."

With a sinking heart, I turned around to see James and Bridget standing next to each other in the entrance to the living room.

"You remember Charlie, don't you?" Blanche was saying, and I nodded to both of them as she introduced Pat and Tiki.

Of course, Bridget looked amazing. Her long, strawberry-blonde curls were half pulled up away from her face in a loose ponytail, and her green silk blouse perfectly matched her eyes. Her jeans were tight, and she had paired them with impossibly high heels. "Oh," she exclaimed when she saw Tiki on the couch. She toddled over to the little dog, moving surprisingly fast in those shoes. "How precious." Tiki wagged her tail politely.

James, on the other hand, looked like he had been ridden hard and put away wet. His hair was standing straight up, as though he had been constantly running his hands through it, and he badly needed a shave. His smile was perfunctory and didn't reach his eyes, which were puffy, as if he were nursing a hangover.

"How was lunch?" Blanche asked, before catching my gaze. "Bridget wanted to cheer James up, so she took him out to eat."

"Overall, it was fine, but they overcooked James's steak sandwich. I told him to send it back, but he refused," Bridget said, sharing a look with Blanche.

"I wasn't that hungry, anyway," James answered, his tone brusque while his eyes met mine. "Wait, now I remember you. You're Anastasia's Bride Whisperer."

"I am," I said.

There was desperation in his gaze. "Have you seen Anastasia?"

"I have," I said as Blanche placed her china cup down on the table. "She misses you."

"I miss her, too," James said at the same time as Blanche started to talk. "James, I really don't think this is the time ..."

James ignored her. "How is she? And where is she? Is she here in Redemption, or did they move her to another jail?"

"She's home," I said, shooting a sideways glance at Blanche, who was looking more and more unnerved. "She got out on bail earlier today."

James closed his eyes. "Oh, thank goodness." His eyes popped back open. "I need to go see her."

"No, James." Blanche stood up. "We talked about this. You can't."

"Why not?" he asked, raking his hand through his hair. "She's my fiancé."

"She's being investigated for murdering her wedding planner," Blanche said, moving quickly toward him.

"Which is why she needs my support," James countered.

Blanche put a hand on his arm. "James, remember what the lawyer told us."

Lawyer? I turned sideways to meet Pat's gaze, which looked as surprised as I felt. Why would they be talking to a lawyer? Did they know more than they were saying?

Or was it just a case of wealthy people consulting their lawyer "just because"?

"It's better to stay out of it, at least until the investigation is over," Blanche continued. "We don't want to taint anything."

"There's nothing to taint," James said. "She didn't do it."

Blanche's gaze softened. "Now, James ..."

James yanked his arm away. "I told you, she couldn't possibly do anything like that."

"Well, we need to let the police do their job," she said. "You don't want to do anything that ends up getting her in more trouble, do you?"

James backed up, the tension in his body visible. "No, of course not, but ..."

"I agree with your mother," I said. Both Blanche and James looked at me. "You should keep your distance. Just for now. You don't want to compromise the investigation. Let's see what happens and what the police find out. Then, you can talk to her."

"Yes, listen to Charlie," Blanche said, her expression grateful.

James didn't seem to echo the sentiment as he gnawed on his bottom lip, clearly agitated. "Fine," he said. "If you think it's better for Anastasia, I won't contact her."

"I do," I said.

"Can you at least get a message to her?"

"Of course," I said sweetly. Blanche's face hardened. She didn't look nearly as grateful anymore, but it was clear she knew not to protest.

"Can you tell her I miss her? And I love her? And as soon as this all gets sorted out, we're going to have the best wedding ever?"

Blanche closed her eyes.

I smiled at him. "Absolutely, I will."

Chapter 11

"Is Anastasia here?" I asked Dana when she opened the front door. I was reassured to see that her grooming habits had returned, as she was right back to resembling Princess Di rather than, well, something more like me.

Dana's eyes widened. "Why? Do you have news?"

"In a way," I said. "I have a message from James."

"Oh." Dana's expression was a mixture of disappointment and relief. "Yes, she's in the living room. She'll love to hear it. Nice to see you, Pat. And Tiki."

"Likewise," Pat said. After leaving Blanche, we had driven straight to Dana's from Riverview. I figured the sooner I could give Anastasia a little good news, the better. "I'm so sorry about all of this," Pat continued as we both stepped inside.

Dana's expression changed to resignation. "Yeah, well, it's tough." She shut the door behind us. "Did Blanche say anything about Jane?"

"Nothing other than she didn't really know Jane at all," I answered.

Dana wrinkled her nose at me. "What do you mean? She recommended her to us."

"True, but I guess she didn't know Jane personally. Some friends of hers had hired Jane for their son's wedding."

Dana's look was confused. "I thought ... well, I guess it doesn't matter. Maybe Anastasia was confused."

"What do you mean?"

Dana looked uncomfortable. "Anastasia had made it sound like Blanche herself had hired Jane at some point ... maybe not to plan a wedding, but some other party. But I suppose it was probably a misunderstanding."

"Probably," I agreed, although I did find it curious. Maybe Anastasia did mix up what she'd heard, but if she didn't, why would Blanche lie?

Was it possible Blanche was hiding her true relationship with Jane?

"Oh, before I forget," Dana was saying, breaking into my thoughts. "I now know which anti-anxiety drug killed Jane."

"Oh? Which was it?"

Dana chewed on her lip. "It was ..." she glanced around, almost as if she expected someone to be hiding around the corner spying on us. Even though no one was there, she leaned in closer to Pat and me. "It was one I actually got for Anastasia," she said in a loud whisper.

My stomach twisted into a giant knot. "I thought she wasn't taking any medications. You said that's why you wanted me to bring the tea."

Dana shook her head. "She wasn't, but ... well, you saw her. She was losing her mind. Not only was she becoming more and more high-strung, but she was getting irrational. Especially when it came to Jane. Don't get me wrong—your tea worked wonders with her. And you were the only one who could calm her down. But her anxiety, frustration, and anger would still ratchet up to extremely high levels when you weren't here. So, I ..." she glanced furtively around. "I went to my doctor. I was desperate, you have to understand. I told him ..." she swallowed hard. "I told him I wanted to try this new anti-anxiety medicine. I had heard good things about it—how it had very few side effects—and I thought it might not be a bad one for Anastasia to try. And then, I would still have my own prescription I could keep taking. I figured Anastasia wouldn't need them after the wedding, and I could tell my doctor they didn't work. We could all just go on like before, then."

I stared at Dana with horror. "Dana, that was ... really dangerous. Never mind the ethics around what you did ... you're not a doctor. You shouldn't be prescribing drugs to your niece."

"I know, I know. It was a risk."

My eyes widened. "A risk? Dana, a woman is dead!"

"I know, and I'm just sick about it." Dana did look ill. But still. How could she have been so stupid?

I opened my mouth, wanting to share those thoughts, but at that moment, Tiki nudged my arm with her little nose. I looked down to see her bright, black eyes looking into mine. She was wearing a purple-and-silver ensemble with matching silver ribbons. I didn't think the silver suited her, but Pat had informed me I was wrong.

I forced myself to take a deep breath. Yelling at Dana about what she did wasn't going to help anything, especially in terms of getting Anastasia out of the mess she'd found herself in. I wondered if the cops knew she had been taking Dana's meds, and that's why they were so confident about arresting her.

"So, what happened? Did Anastasia take the drugs?"

Dana shook her head, her face unhappy. "No. She wanted nothing to do with them. I kept telling her they were safe, but she refused."

"How could you know they were safe? They were new."

"One of the Duckworths told me."

I blinked at Dana. "Blanche?"

"No. I'm blanking on his name." She closed her eyes and pressed her fingers against her temple. "Was it Ted? Ned? Argh, I can't remember now. But he's involved in the company that manufactures them. He told me how excited they were about this new drug, and how they'd had a big breakthrough or something. It was going to revolutionize anti-anxiety medicine, according to him."

"When did you have this conversation?" I asked.

"At Anastasia's engagement party," Dana said. "There were a few of them there. It was in Riverview, at their club. It was quite nice. They had rented out the dining room ..."

I waved my hand to stop her. "You're saying you heard about this anti-anxiety drug at Anastasia's engagement party, and you remembered it enough to ask your doctor about it?"

She looked ashamed. "Not exactly. He gave me his card, so when I decided I needed to get a prescription, I called him to ask him more questions. He was so kind. Even sent some samples to my doctor."

"I bet," I said faintly, thinking I would call a pharmaceutical representative a lot of things, but "kind" wasn't one of them.

"Anyway, I wanted you to know." Dana looked dejected, as if she knew how this little detail could be spun to trap Anastasia in an ever-deepening web of presumed guilt. "Charlie, you have to find out what really happened. She can't go to jail because of me. I already feel so guilty over Jane's death. I don't think I could stand it if Anastasia went to jail just because I was trying to help her."

Her expression was so forlorn, I didn't want to make her feel any worse, but I also couldn't offer her any false promises. Instead, I reached out and squeezed her arm. "I'm going to do everything I can to help Anastasia. I promise."

Dana let out a big, shuddering sigh before glancing up at me with a smile. "I knew I could count on you. Shall we go find Anastasia and tell her James's message?"

* * *

I suppose it wasn't surprising that Anastasia burst into tears again after I delivered the message from James. I left her in the capable hands of Pat, Mary Rose, and Dana while I hurried to the kitchen to make tea.

Cyndi was there, spreading peanut butter and honey on graham crackers. She looked at me with that disdainful glare teenagers are prone to throw at adults. "She's not a bride anymore, you know," she said, licking the honey off her wrist. "So she doesn't need a Bride Whisperer."

I moved to the stove to get the water boiling. "Well, now I'm helping her stay out of jail, so maybe I'm a Jailbird Whisperer."

Cyndi let out a harsh cackle as she doused the graham crackers with honey. "Well, if that's what you are, she *is* going to need you." She ran a finger around the pool of honey on the plate. "She's screwed."

Unfortunately, I sort of agreed with her assessment, although I was a little surprised at how callous she was being, even for a snotty teenager. "It doesn't bother you that your cousin might be going to jail for murder? And a woman died in your back-yard?"

Cyndi stabbed the knife into the peanut butter, her move-ments uncharacteristically vicious. "Why should I care about that? No one cares about anything I think, anyway."

I studied her as I started digging through the cupboards for a mug. Maybe I'd misunderstood what I had first seen. It wasn't apathy in her reaction, but anger. "Actually, I'd love to hear what you think."

Cyndi eyed me suspiciously. "You're just saying that."

"No, I really mean it. The only reason I didn't ask sooner is because I didn't think you were here during the shower. I didn't see you anywhere. Were you around?"

I assumed her answer would be no, but since she didn't im-mediately respond, it was clear Cyndi had something to get off her chest. I figured this would be the best way to keep the con-versation going. With any luck, she had seen something that might be helpful. Maybe she'd noticed Jane pawing through her mother's medicine cabinet the day before the shower, or some-thing. Of course, it was also possible she just needed to talk.

To my surprise, Cyndi said she *was* around. She was sup-posed to have gone to the movies with a friend, but that friend had gotten sick, so Cyndi basically hid out in her room. "That's all my mother wanted to talk about. She never asked me what was going on in my life, anymore. It was just Anastasia, Anasta-sia, Anastasia."

"That's rough," I said sympathetically. "Especially since An-astasia has a mother."

"I know, right?" Cyndi agreed. "Why couldn't Aunt Mary Rose be more involved? Why does my mother always have to end up taking charge? It was so frustrating. And everything about that wedding was drama. Drama, drama, drama. The last thing I wanted was to go to that stupid shower. So, when Faye told me she couldn't make the movies, I wasn't about to tell my mother. She was already upset with me for not wanting to be there, so I knew if she found out Faye canceled, I'd be stuck going."

I couldn't believe my luck. Cyndi was in her bedroom during the party. "I don't suppose you happened to notice anyone come upstairs who wasn't supposed to?"

"What, like Anastasia sneaking around my mother's medicine cabinet to grab the drugs?" She shot me a sarcastic smile. "No, nothing like that."

Her answer surprised me. "You truly think your cousin killed Jane?"

Cyndi shrugged. "Who knows? She certainly was angry enough with Jane to kill her. Although I guess it would be more likely for her to have done something in the heat of the moment, like hit her or shove her down the stairs. Poisoning her champagne glass seems a little premeditated."

I had been measuring tea while Cyndi was talking, but at the mention of the champagne, I paused. "Champagne? Do they know that's how Jane was poisoned? From the champagne?"

Cyndi took a huge bite of the graham cracker/peanut butter/honey concoction, brushing the crumbs off her bottom lip. "I just assumed," she said, her mouth full.

"Why would you assume that?"

"Because I saw Jane drinking champagne right before she collapsed."

The tea kettle started to whistle, startling me. I quickly moved it to a cooler burner as Cyndi took another bite. "Wait a minute. You said you weren't at the party."

"I wasn't. I was in my room."

Teenagers. No wonder no one had asked her if she saw or knew anything. It was like pulling teeth, to drag information out of her.

"Then how do you know she was drinking champagne before she collapsed?"

Cyndi's eyes flickered toward me. "Because my bedroom window overlooks the party." Her voice was so low, it was hard to hear her. She glared at her graham cracker concoction before dropping it back on the plate, wiping the crumbs from her fingers.

I took a step closer. "Are you saying you saw Jane die?"

She glanced up at me again, her expression bitter. "Would you care if I did?"

"Of course I would."

She went back to brooding at her snack. I stayed quiet, waited for her to continue. Finally, she did. "I saw Jane pick up a glass of champagne from the table, take a few sips, and then collapse. At the time, I didn't think anything of it. I figured she just had too much to drink." Her lips twisted into a sardonic smile. "It wouldn't be the first time, that's for sure. It wasn't until I heard the commotion and saw the EMTs arrive that I began to realize it might be more serious. And then, when I heard she died in the hospital ..." her voice trailed away.

"Cyndi, you have to tell the cops what you saw," I said.

She shook her head violently. "I can't."

"Why not?"

She kept shaking her head. "Because ... everything. My mother would know I lied. That I didn't say anything right away. Can't you tell them?"

I moved over to the table to sit down next to her. She seemed to have shrunk, curling in on herself as she kept her gaze down. "I know it's scary, but you have to do this. Think how you will feel if Anastasia ends up being convicted, and you might have been able to prevent it."

She was rocking back and forth. "Maybe. I don't know."

I wanted to reach out to comfort her, but I wasn't sure how she would react. "Did you see where the champagne came from?"

She paused her rocking. "I'm not sure. It was just sitting there, on the table, I think."

"Where on the table? Do you remember?"

"At the head. Where Anastasia would have been sitting."

I jerked back. The champagne was sitting at Anastasia's place? "Are you sure?"

Cyndi nodded. "Positive. I remember, because it was the only glass of champagne on the table. Everyone else was holding theirs. And Jane walked by, real casual like, and snatched it up. Like she was pretending she was clearing off the table or something." Cyndi shook her head, a disgusted look on her face. "She was always doing that. Finishing off other people's glasses of champagne. So gross."

"Yeah, I agree it's a gross habit," I said. I couldn't help but wonder if that very gross habit was what ended up getting her killed.

Chapter 12

"Charlie! What a surprise!" Blanche stood at her front door. She had changed into a simple-but-elegant black dress, and I wondered if I was interrupting anything. "I wasn't expecting you."

"I know. I took a chance and stopped by. I hope that's okay? I promise I only need a minute."

After I left Dana's, I couldn't stop thinking about everything I had learned. I especially couldn't stop thinking about Jane nabbing a glass of champagne from the table. The more I thought about it, the more I wondered if Jane was even the target.

Was it possible someone else at the party was the intended victim—maybe even Anastasia, seeing as how the glass was at her place at the table—but for some reason, rather than drinking the champagne, it was left it on the table, only for Jane to scoop up?

Or perhaps Jane WAS the target, and whoever wanted her dead knew her habit of scarfing down abandoned alcoholic drinks.

Too many possibilities. I could just picture Wyle's expression when he learned he suddenly had far more potential victims, and suspects, than he did before.

Speaking of Wyle, I felt a little pang of guilt that I hadn't talked to him yet. I had intended to call him when I left Dana's house, but instead found myself driving back to Riverview after dropping Pat off, who was bitterly disappointed she wasn't able to go with me. Unfortunately, she had plans with Richard to get ready for.

Blanche glanced at the slim, diamond-encrusted watch on her wrist. "It's getting a little late. I do have a dinner engagement, but ..." she frowned for a moment as she considered the possibilities. I could almost see her curiosity winning her internal battle. She pushed the door open wider. "I have a few minutes. I'm guessing it's pretty important."

"It is." The one detail that kept circling around in my head was how every time I turned around, a Duckworth popped up.

It couldn't be a coincidence.

She led me back to the living room, and we settled back into our respective positions—her on the sofa and me perched on a chair. "So, what's going on? Did something happen to Anastasia?"

Rather than answer her, I asked my own question. "Did you know that Anastasia was taking a very new anti-anxiety medicine that was created in a pharmaceutical company your family owns?" A little lie, yes, but I was crossing my fingers that Blanche wouldn't realize it.

She shifted on the couch. "We don't own it, per se. My family has a controlling interest, yes, but we don't own it."

"Okay. But one of your family members told Dana about a new anti-anxiety drug Anastasia could try." I was still stretching the truth, but I wanted to get her reaction.

"I didn't realize Anastasia needed anti-anxiety medication."

"But you must have seen how stressed she was, planning the wedding."

Blanche gave me a pointed look. "Well, I figured that's what YOU were for."

Touché. "Well, yes, I was. But sometimes, people need something a little stronger than tea."

She almost smiled. "I suspect in many cases, prescription drugs are more effective than tea. No offense, of course."

I smiled widely. "None taken."

She shifted again. "Is Anastasia having some sort of reaction to the anti-anxiety medicine? Is that why you're here? I'm afraid that's nothing I would know how to deal with, but I can certainly give you the name of our attorney." She started to move, like she was about to get up.

"No, Anastasia is fine."

Her expression was perplexed. "Then I'm afraid I don't understand why you're here."

I leaned forward, like I was about to share a juicy secret. "It's just the police have discovered that Anastasia's anti-anxiety drugs were what killed Jane."

Blanche's eyes went wide. "Really? Jane died of an overdose?"

"It sure looks that way."

"And it was Anastasia's prescription drugs." Blanche shook her head slowly, clucking her tongue. "Such a shame. I blame myself."

I tilted my head. "Why?"

Blanche sighed. "Because I saw the signs, and I should have done something." She shook her head sadly. "I could see Anastasia was struggling. Planning this wedding was clearly too much for her. I should have stepped in ... maybe offered to take some of the planning off her shoulders. But I thought as the bride, she would want to be involved in every decision, so I chose not to say anything. But now I wonder ... if I had said or done something, maybe Jane would be alive right now."

"So you think Anastasia snapped?"

"Unfortunately, yes. It happens."

"Even though she was on anti-anxiety medication?"

"Alas, prescription drugs aren't a magic wand, even if they seem like it at times. Especially anti-anxiety and other mental-health drugs. They can take some time to stabilize the person, which is something Anastasia may not have had. It's also possible she wasn't on the right dose, or that specific drug wasn't right for her. Like I said, when it comes to mental health, there's not always a quick fix. So, to answer your question, yes, Anastasia still could have snapped the morning of the shower, and in a fit of some delusion, dumped her pills into Jane's champagne glass. It's very sad, but possible."

"Yes, it is sad," I said, crossing my legs. "It's also surprising."

Blanche's expression was mildly curious. "How so?"

"Well, I don't know how Anastasia would know which champagne glass was Jane's. It's not like Jane should have been drinking at all, considering she was working."

Blanche shifted in her seat again. "That's true, but as we all know, Jane did have a nasty little habit around alcohol, didn't she?"

"Yes, that's true. But if someone just snaps, would she have the wherewithal to just wait until she could find an abandoned champagne glass somewhere? Doesn't that seem a little premeditated, to you? Anastasia would have had to find the glass and dump the drugs into it, unnoticed. And she would basically be risking any number of people other than Jane picking it up and ingesting it."

A tiny smile played at Blanche's lips. "Not if it was Anastasia's champagne."

I blinked at her. "I'm sorry? You think Anastasia drugged her own champagne glass?"

"Why not? It's perfect. She'd be holding the glass, so she could easily add the drugs without anyone seeing. Then, she could casually set it on the table at the right time, knowing Jane would snatch it up the moment she walked by. Brilliant, really."

My mind whirled, picturing that day in my mind. *Anastasia holding the glass of champagne and talking to Bridget. Anastasia's champagne glass untouched as she eagerly takes my tea.*

And just like that, it all fell into place.

I flashed Blanche a sweet little smile. "You're right. It *was* brilliant."

Blanched smiled, nodding her head.

"There's only one thing," I continued, before narrowing my eyes. "I never said that Jane was drugged with the champagne. Nor did I say where she picked up the glass."

Blanche's smile disappeared. Her jaw went slack. She stared at me for a moment, uncomprehending. "Well … well … you must have," she stuttered. "How else would I know?"

"That's a good question," I said.

"Maybe the cops told me."

"I doubt the cops would say that to you, or anyone else, for that matter, but not Anastasia," I said.

"Well, if the cops didn't tell you, how do *you* know?" she demanded.

"Because I have an eyewitness," I said bluntly.

Blanche's face went white. Her mouth worked, but no sound came out.

From behind, I heard the slam of a door. "Honey? Blanche? Sorry I'm late," a male voice called out as heavy footsteps sounded on the floor. "It was one thing after another at the office. Are you ready … oh. Hello. I didn't realize you had company."

Blanche finally got her mouth to work. "I think you should leave," she said in a raspy whisper.

I nodded and stood up, turning to see the perplexed expression on James Senior's face. "Am I interrupting something?"

"Nothing at all," I said cheerfully. "I'll see myself out."

Chapter 13

"I still can't get over the fact that a Duckworth killed a wedding planner," Pat said. We were back in my kitchen, cups of tea and cookies in front of us. Next to us, Midnight snoozed on a chair in the warm sun while Tiki looked expectantly at Pat for a bite of cookie.

"Never underestimate a Duckworth. If they perceive one of their own is marrying beneath them, they'll do pretty much anything," I said. "And it seems Blanche didn't consider Anastasia a suitable bride for her only son."

"I guess," Pat said thoughtfully, as she broke off a piece of cookie for Tiki. "Unfortunately for Blanche, her plan didn't work."

"Yeah, karma can be a brutal mistress," I said.

Despite all of Blanche's scheming, it appeared all that she really accomplished was landing herself in legal hot water and solidifying the relationship between her son and Anastasia. Clearly not what she had in mind.

If James and Anastasia weren't married yet, they would be soon. They had decided against the big wedding and ran off to Vegas to elope.

"Although it's a bummer we now all have to suffer," Pat said with an exaggerated sigh. "No Redemption Supper Club reception for any of us."

"Actually, it's possible they'll have a party there later to celebrate the wedding," I said. Dana had told me they weren't able to get their deposit back, but they were able to renegotiate the contract.

At that, Pat perked up. I debated whether or not to tell her the renegotiated event wasn't going to be nearly as elaborate— no sit-down dinner ... just drinks and appetizers. I decided that could wait until the event was finalized.

"So, what I keep going back to is who Blanche was actually trying to kill," Pat said, feeding Tiki another piece of cookie. "She put the drugs in Anastasia's champagne glass, right? So was she trying to kill Anastasia or the wedding planner?"

"I honestly don't know," I said. "Blanche isn't saying one way or the other. My guess is she figured one of them, either Jane or Anastasia, would drink the champagne, and regardless of which one did, the wedding would be off. If Anastasia drank it and died, her death would be ruled an accidental overdose, and everyone would say she shouldn't have mixed alcohol with her anti-anxiety medicine. And if it was Jane, Anastasia would be the prime suspect."

"Which she was," Pat said. "It's amazing that her plan almost worked."

"Almost," I said, as an image of an angry and hurt Cyndi flashed in my mind. "Good thing Cyndi's movie plans were canceled."

"And good thing you took the time to listen to her," Pat said.

"Well, I suspect Wyle would eventually have figured it out," I said. "But yes, I'm glad it all worked out in the end."

Pat made a face at me. "I don't know about that. But you're right ... all is well that ends well. True love wins out. But more importantly, we still get to celebrate in style at the Redemption Supper Club."

I held up my mug in a toast. "Hear, hear."

A Note From Michele

Can't get enough of Charlie? I've got you covered. Keep going with *Three French Hens and a Murder*, coming December 2023!

And don't forget to check out audio! The entire series is available on Audible on audio. Or you can also start from the beginning with Book 1 *The Murder Before Christmas*.

A dead husband. A pregnant wife. A poisoned Christmas gift. Can Charlie discover the grinch who stole Christmas?

Grab your copy here:

MPWnovels.com/r/bwedxmaswide

* * *

You can also check out exclusive bonus content for the Charlie Kingsley Mystery series. Here's the link:

MPWnovels.com/r/wedding-to-murder-bonus

The bonus content reveals hints, clues, and sneak peeks you won't get just by reading the books, so you'll definitely want to take a look. You're going to discover a side of Redemption that is only available here.

* * *

If you enjoyed A Wedding to Murder For, it would be wonderful if you would take a few minutes to leave a review and rating on Goodreads:

goodreads.com/book/show/136307892-a-wedding-to-murder-for

or Bookbub:

bookbub.com/books/a-wedding-to-murder-for-charlie-kingsley-mysteries-by-michele-pariza-wacek

(Feel free to follow me on any of those platforms as well.) I thank you and other readers will thank you (as your reviews will help other readers find my books.)

The *Charlie Kingsley Mysteries* series is a spin-off from my award-winning *Secrets of Redemption* series. *Secrets of Redemption* is a little different from the *Charlie Kingsley Mysteries*, as it's more psychological suspense, but it's still clean like a cozy.

You can learn more about both series, including how they fit together, at MPWNovels.com, along with lots of other fun things such as short stories, deleted scenes, giveaways, recipes, puzzles and more.

I've also included a sneak peek of *The Murder Before Christmas*, just turn the page to get started

Murder Before Christmas Chapter 1

"So, Courtney, is it?" I asked with what I hoped was a comforting and nonthreatening smile. I set the mug holding my newest tea blend I'd created for the Christmas season—a variety of fresh mint and a couple of other secret ingredients—down on the kitchen table. I called it "Candy Cane Concoctions", and hoped others would find it as soothing as it was refreshing. "What can I do for you?"

Courtney didn't look at me as she reached for her tea. She was young, younger than me, and extremely pretty, despite looking like something the cat dragged in. (And believe me, I know all about what cats can drag in. Midnight, my black cat, had presented me with more than my share of gifts over the years.) Courtney's long, wavy blonde hair was pulled back in a haphazard ponytail, and there were puffy, black circles under her china-blue eyes. She was also visibly pregnant.

"Well, Mrs. Kingsley," she began, but I quickly interrupted her.

"It's Miss, but please, call me Charlie." Yes, she was younger than me, but for goodness sake, not THAT much younger. Maybe it was time to start getting more serious about my morning makeup routine.

Her lips quirked up in a tiny smile that didn't quite reach her eyes. "Charlie, then. I was hoping you could make me a love potion."

I quickly dropped my gaze, busying myself by pushing the plate of frosted Christmas sugar cookies I had made earlier toward her, not wanting her to see my shock and sorrow. She was pregnant and wanted a love potion. This just couldn't be good.

"I don't actually do love potions," I said. "I make custom-blended teas and tinctures."

Her eyebrows knit together in confusion. "But people have been raving about how much you've helped them. Mrs. Witmore swears you cured her thyroid problems."

I tried not to sigh. "My teas and tinctures do have health benefits, that's true. Certain herbs and flowers can help with common ailments. In fact, for much of human civilization, there were no prescription drugs, so all they had to use were herbs and flowers. But I can't promise any cures."

"What about Ruthie?" Courtney asked. "She claims those heart tinctures you made are the reason Bob finally noticed her."

I gritted my teeth. When Ruthie's dad was recovering from a heart attack, I made a couple of teas and tinctures for him. Ruthie, who had a crush on her coworker Bob for years, was apparently so desperate for him to notice her that one day, she decided to bring one of my tinctures to work (I'm unclear which) and slip it into his drink. And apparently, shortly after that, Bob started up a conversation with her, and eventually asked her out on a date.

It didn't help matters that Jean, Ruthie's mother, had claimed my tinctures had reignited her and her husband's love life, which is probably how Ruthie got the idea to try them with Bob in the first place.

Needless to say, that was an unintended benefit.

"I didn't give Ruthie a love potion," I said. "I gave her dad some tinctures and teas to help his heart."

Courtney gazed at me with those clear-blue eyes, reminding me of a broken-down, worn-out doll. "Well, isn't that where love starts?"

"Maybe," I said. "But my intention was to heal her father's heart, not to make anyone fall in love with anyone else."

"But it worked," she said. "Can you just sell me whatever you gave her? I have money. I'll pay."

"It's not that simple," I said. "I really need to ask you some questions. It's always good to talk to your doctor, as well."

She bit her lip and dropped her gaze to the tea in her hands. She looked so lost and alone, I felt sorry for her.

"Why don't you tell me a little bit about who you want this love potion for?" I asked. "That would help me figure out how best to help you."

She didn't immediately answer, instead keeping her eyes down. Just as I was starting to think she wasn't going to say anything at all, she spoke. "It's for my husband," she said, her voice so low, it was nearly a whisper.

I could feel my heart sink to the floor. This was even more heartbreaking than I had imagined. "You think your husband fell out of love with you?"

"I know he has," she said. "He's having an affair."

"Oh Courtney," I sighed. "I'm so sorry to hear that."

She managed a tiny nod and picked up her tea to take a sip.

"Have you two talked about it?"

She shook her head quickly.

"Does he know you know?"

She shrugged.

"Maybe that's the place to start," I said, keeping my voice gentle. "Having a conversation."

"It won't help," she said, her voice still quiet.

"How do you know if you haven't tried?"

She didn't answer ... just stared into her tea.

"Have you thought about marriage counseling?"

"He won't go." Her voice was firm.

"Have you asked?"

"I know. He's said before he thinks therapy is a waste of money."

"Okay. But you have a baby on the way," I said. "You need to be able to talk through things. I understand it might be difficult to talk about something like *this*, but ..."

"He's in love with her." The words burst out of her as she raised her head. The expression on her face was so anguished that for a moment, it took my breath away.

"But how do you know if you haven't talked to him about it?"

"I just do," she said. "When you're married, you know these things. You can sense when your husband has fallen out of love with you. Hence, my need for a love potion. I need him to fall back in love with me. You can see how urgent this is." She gestured to her stomach. "In a few months, we're going to have a baby. I just *have* to get him to fall back in love with me."

Oh man, this was not going well. "I see why you would think that would be easier, but the problem is, there's no such thing as a love potion."

"Can you please just sell me what you made for Ruthie's dad? So I can at least try?"

"Whatever happened between Ruthie and Bob had nothing to do with one of my tinctures," I said flatly. "I don't want to give you false hope. I really think your best course of action is to have an open and honest conversation with him about the affair."

She was noticeably disappointed. It seemed to radiate out of every pore. I hated being the one to cause that, but I also wasn't going to sell her anything that could be misconstrued as a "love potion." Not only for her sake, but my own. The last thing I needed was lovesick women showing up at my door to buy something that didn't exist.

"Okay," she said quietly as she ducked her head so I couldn't quite see her face. "No love potion. How about the opposite?"

I looked at her in confusion. "The opposite?"

"Yes. Something that would kill him."

My mouth fell open. "Wha ... I'm sorry, could you repeat that?" I must have heard her wrong. She was still talking so quietly, not to mention hiding her face.

Courtney blinked and looked up at me. "I'm sorry?"

"I didn't hear what you said. Could you repeat it?"

"Oh. It was nothing." She offered an apologetic smile.

"No, really," I said. "I thought ..." I laughed a little self-consciously. "I thought you said you wanted something to kill your husband."

She blinked again. "Oh. Yeah. It was just a joke."

"A joke?"

"Yeah. I mean, you know. Sometimes married people want to kill each other. No big deal." Now it was her turn to let out a little twitter of laughter. "Have you ever been married?"

I shivered and put my hands around my mug to absorb the warmth. "No." Which was true. I had never been officially married, but that didn't mean my love life wasn't ... complicated.

Nor did it mean I didn't know exactly what she was talking about.

"Well, you know, sometimes married people can just get really angry with each other, and in the heat of the moment, even want to kill each other," she explained. "But they don't mean it. It's just because they love each other so much that sometimes that passion looks like something else. In the heat of the moment, in the middle of a fight, you can say all sorts of things you don't mean. But of course, they wouldn't *do* anything about it."

"Of course," I said. I decided not to mention that when she said it, she wasn't actually arguing with her husband. Nor did I bring up how perhaps she was protesting a bit too much.

I gave her a hard look as I sipped my tea.

She kept her gaze firmly on the table, refusing to meet my eyes. "Did I tell you how wonderful this blend is?" she asked. "It's so refreshing. Reminds me of a candy cane."

"Thanks. It's called 'Candy Cane Concoctions,' actually. I created it for the holidays," I said.

"It's wonderful." She took another hurried drink and put her mug down, tea sloshing over the side. "Are you selling it? Could I buy some?"

"Sure," I said, getting up from my chair. "Hang on a minute. I'll get you a bag."

She nodded as I left the kitchen to head upstairs to my office/work room. Although, to be fair, it was so small, it wasn't uncommon to find drying herbs or plants throughout the house.

I collected a bag and headed back to the kitchen. When I walked in, Courtney was standing up, fiddling with her purse. I instantly felt like something was off. Maybe it was the way she was standing or the bend of her neck, but she oozed guilt.

"Oh, there you are," she said, fishing out her wallet. "How much do I owe you?'

I told her, and she pulled out a wad of cash, handing me a twenty.

"I'll have to get you some change," I said.

"That's not necessary," she said, taking the bag. "You were so helpful to me, and besides, I need to get going."

"But this is way too much," I protested. "Just let me find my purse."

She waved me off as she left the kitchen and headed for the front door. "Nonsense. Truly, you were very helpful. No change is necessary." She jammed her arms into her coat, and without bothering to zip it up, opened the front door and headed out into the cold.

I closed the door after her, watching her through the window as she made her way down the driveway and into her car. She didn't seem very steady on her feet, and I wanted to make sure she got into her vehicle safely. After she drove off, I went back to the kitchen to look around.

Nothing appeared to be out of order. If she had been digging around looking for something (like something to kill her husband with), it wasn't obvious.

Still, I couldn't shake that uneasy feeling.

I went to the table to collect the dishes. Midnight strolled in as I was giving myself a pep talk.

"I'm sure she didn't mean it," I said to him. "She was probably just upset. I mean, she wasn't getting her love potion, and clearly, she was uncomfortable having a conversation with her husband. Although you'd think that would be a red flag."

Midnight sat down, his dark-green eyes studying me.

"Of course, that's hardly my business," I continued. "She's upset with him, and rightfully so. Who wouldn't be? Even if she wasn't actually joking in the moment, she was surely just letting off steam."

Midnight's tail twitched.

"Maybe this was even the first time she said it out loud," I said as I moved to the sink. "And now that she said it, she realized how awful it was. Of course she would never do anything like that." I turned to the cat. "Right?"

Midnight started cleaning himself.

"You're a lot of help," I muttered, turning back to the sink to finish the washing up.

As strange as that encounter was, it was likely the end of it. I hoped.

Want to keep reading? Grab your copy of **The Murder Before Christmas** here:

MPWNovels.com/r/bwedxmaswide

More *Charlie Kingsley Mysteries:* (cozy mysteries)
A Grave Error (a free prequel novel)
The Murder Before Christmas (Book 1)
Ice Cold Murder (Book 2)
Murder Next Door (Book 3)
The Murder of Sleepy Hollow (Book 5)
Red Hot Murder (Book 6)
A Cornucopia of Murder (Book 7)
Arson, Old Lace and Murder (Book 8)
Masquerading as Murder (Book 9)
A Wedding to Murder For (novella)
Loch Ness Murder (novella)
Three French Hens and a Murder (novella)
A Room for Murder (novella)

The Redemption Detective Agency: (cozy mysteries)
The Mysterious Case of the Missing Motive

Riverview Mysteries: (psychological thrillers)
The Stolen Twin
The Taking
Mirror Image
The Thirs Nanny
Today I'll See Her (short story)

Secrets of Redemption *series:* (psychological thrillers)
It Began With a Lie (Book 1)
This Happened to Jessica (Book 2)
The Evil That Was Done (Book 3)
The Summoning (Book 4)
The Reckoning (Book 5)
The Girl Who Wasn't There (Book 6)
The Room at the Top of the Stairs (Book 7)
The Search (Book 8)
What Wasn't Forgotten (Book 9)
The Secret Diary of Helen Blackstone (novella)

Access your free exclusive bonus scenes from *A Wedding to Murder For* right here:
MPWnovels.com/r/wedding-to-murder-bonus

About Michele

A USA Today Bestselling, award-winning author, Michele taught herself to read at 3 years old because she wanted to write stories so badly. It took some time (and some detours) but she does spend much of her time writing stories now. Mystery stories, to be exact. They're clean and twisty, and range from psychological thrillers to cozies, with a dash of romance and supernatural thrown into the mix. If that wasn't enough, she posts lots of fun things on her blog, including short stories, puzzles, recipes and more, at MPWNovels.com.

Michele grew up in Wisconsin, (hence why all her books take place there), and still visits regularly, but she herself escaped the cold and now lives in the mountains of Prescott, Arizona with her husband and southern squirrel hunter Cassie.

When she's not writing, she's usually reading, hanging out with her dog, or watching the Food Network and imagining she's an awesome cook. (Spoiler alert, she's not. Luckily for the whole family, Mr. PW is in charge of the cooking.)